核心 素養
108課綱

讀出英品

核心素養 ③

九大技巧打造閱讀力

跨領域主題 ✕ 生活化體裁 ✕ 250道閱讀題

精準貼合108 課綱　高效培養核心素養
用英語打造閱讀、分析、整合力！

作者●Owain Mckimm　　譯者●黃詩韻／劉嘉珮　　審訂●Helen Yeh

Contents

體裁 / 主題	議題	素養
advertisements 廣告 / travel 旅遊	global ocean 海洋教育	semiotics 符號運用
letter 信件 / relationships 人際關係	family education 家庭教育	expression 溝通表達
diary 日記 / animals 動物	morality 道德教育	moral praxis 道德實踐
instant message 即時通訊 / sport 體育	life 生命教育	physical and mental wellness 身心素質
letter 信件 / inspiration for teens 青少年啟發	life 生命教育	interpersonal relationships 人際關係
news clip 新聞短片 / information 資訊	information 資訊教育	media literacy 媒體素養
advertisements 廣告 / houses & apartments 房屋與寓所	information 資訊教育	semiotics 符號運用
obituary 訃聞 / life 生活	life 生命教育	interpersonal relationships 人際關係
poem 詩 / inspiration for teens 青少年啟發	outdoor education 戶外教育	self-advancement 自我精進
passage 文章 / arts & literature 藝術與文學	multiculturalism 多元文化教育	artistic appreciation 藝術涵養

Unit 2　Word Study 字彙學習

體裁 / 主題	議題	素養
speech 演說 / school life 學校生活	life 生命教育	expression 溝通表達
magazine article 雜誌文章 / environment 環境	environment 環境教育	logical thinking 系統思考
blog 部落格 / culture 文化	multiculturalism 多元文化教育	innovation and adaptation 創新應變
interview 訪談 / relationships 人際關係	morality 道德教育	interpersonal relationships 人際關係
passage 文章 / gender equality 性別平等	gender equality 性別平等教育	citizenship 公民意識
conversation 對話 / environment 環境	environment / morality 環境／道德教育	moral praxis 道德實踐
meeting 會議 / business 商業	security 安全教育	teamwork 團隊合作
poster 海報 / animals 動物	information 資訊教育	semiotics 符號運用
instruction 操作說明 / safety 安全	security 安全教育	problem solving 解決問題
video transcripts 影片逐字稿 / relationships 人際關係	international education 國際教育	expression 溝通表達
column 專欄 / relationships 人際關係	life 生命教育	interpersonal relationships 人際關係
instruction 操作說明 / health & body 健康與身體	life 生命教育	physical and mental wellness 身心素質
Q & A 問答 / business 商業	technology 科技教育	semiotics 符號運用
passage 文章 / inspiration for teens 青少年啟發	reading literacy 閱讀素養教育	self-advancement 自我精進

Unit 3 Study Strategies 學習策略

體裁 / 主題	議題	素養
passage 文章 / food & drinks 食物與飲料	multiculturalism 多元文化教育	cultural understanding 多元文化
diary 日記 / nature 自然	outdoor education 戶外教育	problem solving 解決問題
notice 通知單 / school life 學校生活	environment 環境教育	semiotics 符號運用
book foreword 書本前言 / inspiration for teens 青少年啟發	life 生命教育	self-advancement 自我精進
bulletin board 布告欄 / school life 學校生活	reading literacy 閱讀素養教育	expression 溝通表達
passage 文章 / animals / science 動物／科學	environment 環境教育	logical thinking 系統思考

體裁 / 主題	議題	素養
map 地圖 / everyday life 日常生活	rule of law 法治教育	semiotics 符號運用
schedule 時間表 / sport 體育	life 生命教育	physical and mental wellness 身心素質
pie chart 圓餅圖 / business 商業	technology 科技教育	innovation and adaptation 創新應變
bar chart 長條圖 / economy / finance 經濟／財經	life 生命教育	global understanding 國際理解
line chart 折線圖 / travel 旅遊	international education 國際教育	global understanding 國際理解
timeline 時間軸 / politics / laws 政治／法律	international education 國際教育	global understanding 國際理解
table of contents 目錄 / nature 自然	reading literacy / environment 閱讀素養／環境教育	logical thinking 系統思考
website search results 網站搜尋結果 / culture 文化	information 資訊教育	information and technology literacy 科技資訊

體裁 / 主題	議題	素養
thesaurus 索引典 / language & communication 語言與溝通	reading literacy 閱讀素養教育	physical and mental wellness 身心素質
recipe 食譜 / food & drinks 食物與飲料	reading literacy 閱讀素養教育	planning and execution 規劃執行
passage 文章 / holidays & festivals 節日或慶典	multiculturalism 多元文化教育	cultural understanding 多元文化
passage 文章 / famous or interesting people 知名或有趣的人物	human rights 人權教育	global understanding 國際理解
passage 文章 / geography & places 地理與地方	global ocean 海洋教育	global understanding 國際理解
double passages 雙文章 / career 職涯	career planning 生涯規劃教育	problem solving 解決問題
passage 文章 / psychology 心理學	reading literacy 閱讀素養教育	self-advancement 自我精進
conversation 對話 / technology 科技	technology / security 科技／安全教育	interpersonal relationships 人際關係
passage 文章 / safety 安全	security 安全教育	problem solving 解決問題
passage 文章 / nature 自然	environment 環境教育	physical and mental wellness 身心素質
Venn diagram 文氏圖 / sport 體育	multiculturalism 多元文化教育	global understanding 國際理解
index 索引 / arts & literature 藝術與文學	reading literacy 閱讀素養教育	aesthetic literacy 美感素養

Introduction

本套書共四冊，專為英語初學者設計，旨在**增進閱讀理解能力**並**提升閱讀技巧**。全套書符合 108 課綱要旨，強調**跨領域、生活化學習**，文章按照教育部公布的**九大核心素養**與 **19 項議題設計**撰寫，為讀者打造扎實的英語閱讀核心素養能力。

每冊內含 50 篇文章，主題包羅萬象，包括**文化、科學、自然、文學**等，內容以**日常生活常見體裁**寫成，舉凡**電子郵件、邀請函、廣告、公告、對話**皆收錄於書中，以多元主題及多變體裁，豐富讀者閱讀體驗，引導讀者從生活中學習，並將學習運用於生活。每篇文章之後設計**五道閱讀理解題**，依不同閱讀技巧重點精心撰寫，訓練統整、分析及應用所得資訊的能力，同時為日後的國中教育會考做準備。

Key Features 本書特色

1. 按文章難度分級，可依程度選用適合的級數

全套書難度不同，方便各程度的學生使用，以文章字數、高級字詞使用數、文法難度、句子長度分為一至四冊，如下方表格所示：

文章字數（每篇）	國中 1200 字（每篇）	國中 1201–2000 字（每篇）	高中字彙（3–5級）（每篇）	文法	句子最長字數
Book 1 120–150	93%	7 字	3 字	國一	15 字
Book 2 150–180	86%	15 字	6 字	國二	18 字
Book 3 180–210	82%	30 字	7 字	國三	25 字
Book 4 210–250	75%	50 字	12 字	進階	28 字

2. 按文章難度分級，可依程度選用適合的級數

全書**主題多元**，有**青少年生活、家庭、商業、環境、健康、節慶、文化、動物、文學、旅遊**等，帶領讀者以英語探索知識、豐富生活，同時拉近學習與日常的距離。

3. 文章體裁豐富多樣

廣納各類生活中**常見的體裁**，包含**短文、詩篇、對話、廣告、網站、新聞、短片、專欄**等，讓讀者學會閱讀多種體裁文章，將閱讀知識及能力應用於生活中。

4. 外師親錄課文朗讀 MP3

全書文章皆由專業外師錄製 MP3，示範正確發音，促進讀者聽力吸收，提升英文聽力與口說能力。

Structure of the Book | 本書架構

Unit 1 閱讀技巧 Reading Skills

本單元訓練讀者**理解文意**的基本技巧，內容包含：

❶ **歸納要旨／找出支持性細節 Main Ideas / Supporting Details**

要旨是文章傳達的關鍵訊息，也就是作者想要講述的重點。一般而言，只要看前幾句就能大略掌握文章的要旨。

支持性細節就像是築起房屋的磚塊，幫助讀者逐步了解整篇文章要旨，**事實**、**描述**、**比較**、**舉例**都能是支持性細節的一種。

❷ **做出推測／釐清寫作技巧**
Making Inferences / Clarifying Devices

當你在進行**推測**時，需使用已知的資訊去推論出不熟悉的資訊。在篇章的上下文中，讀者藉由文中已提供的資訊去**推測文意**。

作者會想讓自己的文章盡量引人入勝且文意明瞭。當你在閱讀時，需注意作者用**哪些技巧**達到此目的。看看作者是否提供事實及數據？是否向讀者提問？是否舉出例證？仔細閱讀每個句子及段落，試著**分辨寫作技巧**。

❸ **作者的目的及語氣／明辨寫作偏見**
Author's Purpose and Tone / Finding Bias

作者在寫作時通常有**特定的目的**，可能是想博君一笑，或是引發你對某個主題深思。注意作者的**語氣**，他的語氣是詼諧、情感充沛抑或是有耐心的呢？**作者的語氣**可以幫助你找出**作者的目的**。

作者本身的歷練、看法和信仰等因素綜合在一起，就會形成**偏見或特定觀點**。雖然有時難以看出**作者的偏見**，但可從作者的用字以及是否公平陳述兩造論點來窺見端倪。

Unit 2 | 字彙學習 Word Study

本單元訓練讀者**擴充字彙量**，並學會了解文章中的生字，內容包含：

❶ 同義詞與反義詞 Synonyms / Antonyms

在英文中有時兩字的意思相近，此時稱這兩字為**同義詞**；若兩字意思完全相反，則稱為**反義詞**。舉例來說，good（好）和 brilliant（很棒）的意思相近，為同義詞，但 good（好）和 bad（壞）的意思相反，故為反義詞。學習這些詞彙有助提升字彙量，並增進閱讀與寫作能力。

❷ 從上下文推測字義 Words In Context

遇到不會的英文字，就算是跟單字大眼瞪小眼，也無法了解其字義，但若好好觀察此字的**上下文**，或許就能推敲出大略的字義。這項技巧十分重要，尤其有助讀者在閱讀文章時，即使遇到不會的生字，也能選出正確答案。

Unit 3 | 學習策略 Study Strategies

影像圖表與**參考資料**常會附在文章旁，幫助讀者獲得許多額外重點，本單元引導讀者善用文章中的不同素材來蒐集資訊，內容包含：

❶ 影像圖表 Visual Material

影像圖表可以將複雜資訊轉換成簡單的**表格、圖表、地圖**等，是閱讀時的最佳幫手。要讀懂圖表，首先要閱讀**圖表標題與單位**，接著觀察**數值**，只要理解圖表的架構，就能從中得到重要資訊。

❷ 參考資料 Reference Sources

參考資料像是**字典、書籍索引**等，一次呈現大量資訊，能訓練讀者自行追蹤所需重點的能力，並提升讀者對文章的整體理解。

Unit 4 | 綜合練習 Final Review

本單元綜合前三單元內容，幫助讀者回顧全書所學，並藉由文後綜合習題，來檢視自身吸收程度。

How to Use This Book

1 多樣主題增添閱讀樂趣與知識

安全

旅遊

01 A Hotel on Waves

Sail the Seven Seas in Style With Elizabeth Cruises

1 Have you ever dreamed of traveling around the world in luxury? Why not take a relaxing ocean cruise with us? Our modern cruise ships are like floating five-star hotels.

2 During your day you can take a swim in one of two large onboard swimming pools. You can also work out in the onboard gym, or watch a movie in the onboard movie theater. Our many singers, bands, and other performers will keep you entertained during the evening.

3 What's more, our top chefs will prepare three delicious meals for you each day. When you arrive at each destination, we have experienced guides to show you all the best sights and local experiences, food, and culture. So go ahead, book a cruise with us today, and get ready for the best experience of your life!

4 **Here are three amazing cruise packages to choose from.**

European Cruise

Length: 3 weeks
Price per person:
HK$50,000+
Countries visited:
Italy, France, Belgium,
Portugal, Spain, Greece

Asian Cruise

Length: 10 days
Price per person:
HK$25,000+
Countries visited: Japan,
South Korea, Singapore,
Thailand, The Philippines

Caribbean Cruise

Length: 2 weeks
Price per person:
HK$40,000+
Places visited: Jamaica, The
Bahamas, Cayman Islands,
Bermuda, St. Lucia, Belize

5 **Cruises leave year-round from Hong Kong.**

Visit www.elizabethcruises.com for schedules and booking information.

>> When you see someone unconscious, the first step is to tap the person and call an ambulance.

19 6 Steps to Save a Life

1 You find someone unconscious on the floor. What do you do?
Here are six simple steps that you can take to help save that person's life.

2 **Step 1. Call an ambulance**

Tap the person gently and ask if he/she is OK.
If he/she doesn't wake up, call an ambulance right away.

3 **Step 2. Turn the person onto their back**

Carefully, turn the person onto his/her back.
Tilt his/her head back and open his/her mouth.
Look inside. If there is anything there, remove it.

↑ tilting one's head

QUESTIONS

___ 1. **What is the writer's purpose in writing the article?**
(A) To teach the reader something useful.
(B) To help the reader change a bad habit.
(C) To make the reader care about a topic.
(D) To make the reader excited about an event.

___ 2. **What is the main idea of the reading?**
(A) When you perform chest presses, you should always place one hand on top of the other.
(B) If you find someone unconscious, you can save his/her life by following a few easy steps.
(C) If an unconscious person is breathing, you do not have to perform chest presses.
(D) The first thing you should do when you find an unconscious person is call an ambulance.

職涯

Vocational Education

The Next Step

Dear Uncle Mike,

I have a difficult question that I need your help with. I am going to graduate from junior high school next year, but I'm not sure what to do next. Should I try to get into a regular high school and, after that, university? Or should I go to a vocational high school or five-year junior college instead? At a regular high school, the classes are more academic, and at a vocational high school or five-year junior college, the classes are more practical. My parents want me to go to a regular high school. But my passion is working with cars. I think I will get a better education in what I really want to do at a vocational high school or five-year college. What path should I take?

Roy

QUESTIONS

___ 1. **What is Roy's purpose in writing the message?**
(A) To thank Uncle Mike. (B) To ask Uncle Mike for advice.
(C) To offer to help Uncle Mike. (D) To ask about Uncle Mike's job.

___ 2. **What does Roy love to do?**
(A) Do math problems. (B) Paint and draw.
(C) Write stories. (D) Work with cars.

___ 3. **What is probably TRUE about Uncle Mike?**
(A) He does not like to travel. (B) He can fly an airplane.
(C) He likes working with people (D) He wants to quit his job.

2 多元體裁貼近日常閱讀體驗

演講

詩篇

網頁

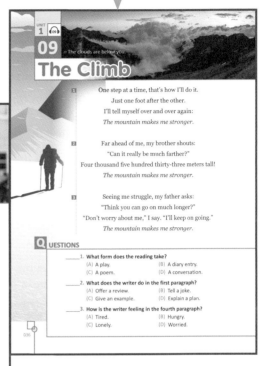

UNIT 1 09

09 The Climb
» The clouds are below you.

1 One step at a time, that's how I'll do it.
Just one foot after the other.
I'll tell myself over and over again:
The mountain makes me stronger.

2 Far ahead of me, my brother shouts:
"Can it really be much farther?"
Four thousand five hundred thirty-three meters tall!
The mountain makes me stronger.

3 Seeing me struggle, my father asks:
"Think you can go on much longer?"
"Don't worry about me," I say. "I'll keep on going."
The mountain makes me stronger.

Q UESTIONS
_____ 1. What form does the reading take?
  (A) A play.   (B) A diary entry.
  (C) A poem.   (D) A conversation.
_____ 2. What does the writer do in the first paragraph?
  (A) Offer a review.   (B) Tell a joke.
  (C) Give an example.   (D) Explain a plan.
_____ 3. How is the writer feeling in the fourth paragraph?
  (A) Tired.   (B) Hungry.
  (C) Lonely.   (D) Worried.

036

UNIT 1 11

11 Goodbye Junior High

1 My fellow students, can you believe that it's been three years already? Just a short time ago we were just silly little kids. Now we are ready for high school!

2 I won't lie: When I arrived here, I was scared. The older kids scared me. **Principal Jackson** *really* scared me! But I soon discovered how kind everyone was, and soon I felt right at home.

3 Our amazing teachers have all worked so hard to give us a good education. They are real heroes. High school will be tough, but our teachers have prepared us well. They have taught us not only their subjects but also how to work hard and never quit. I feel I've learned so much here that my head might explode, just like one of **Mr. Wang**'s crazy science experiments!

4 Many of us will be going to different high schools. We will no longer be together every day. This makes me very sad. But we should also be happy for all the great friends we have made here. No matter where you go from here, know that your junior high school friends will always be there to support you.

5 Thank you, and good luck to everyone for the future!

040
» graduation

UNIT 2 23

23 Exercise Bike for Sale!

For Sale: Second-Hand Exercise Bike

- Model: Superfit 3000
- Made in Germany
- Used but **in very good condition**
- Can **deliver** anywhere in the Boston area.

Price: **$249.99**
(or best offer)

Q A

Question 1
Mike_C:
Hi, this looks great. It might be a bit too big for my apartment, though. What are the bike's measurements?

Answer:
The bike is 1.5 m long and 50 cm wide.

Question 2
Diane_M:
Can I ask how heavy it is? I'm afraid I won't be able to carry it up the stairs in my building.

Answer:
It's 30 kg. It should be fine to carry. But if you need help, I can help you carry it upstairs when I deliver it to you.

066

3 每篇文章後附五道閱讀理解題，訓練培養九大閱讀技巧，包含：

_____ **1. What is Kate's main message to Jack?**
(A) She and her family are going rock climbing this weekend.
(B) He should join her and her family rock climbing this weekend.
(C) Going rock climbing will help him prepare for his math test.
(D) She will send him the details about rock climbing later.

❶ 歸納要旨

_____ **2. Which of the following does rock climbing NOT help develop?**
(A) Your muscles. (B) Your coordination.
(C) Your problem-solving abilities. (D) Your language skills.

❷ 找出支持性細節

_____ **3. Which of the following people is the apartment a good fit for?**
(A) A large family of four.
(B) Someone who likes to live around quiet places.
(C) A fun-loving college student.
(D) Someone who is visiting London for a few months.

❸ 做出推測

_____ **4. What does the writer provide in the fourth paragraph?**
(A) Some suggestions. (B) Some rules.
(C) Some problems. (D) Some jokes.

❹ 釐清寫作技巧

_____ **1. What is the purpose of this magazine article?**
(A) To teach the reader something interesting.
(B) To give the reader an answer to a difficult question.
(C) To show the reader how to do something.
(D) To sell the reader something useful.

❺ 作者的目的及語氣

_____ **2. Which of the following is NOT a biased word in the article?**
(A) Amazing. (B) Ignorant. (C) Poor. (D) Fresh.

❻ 明辨寫作偏見

_____ **1. Which word means the same as "unusual"?**
(A) Common. (B) Strange. (C) Real. (D) Boring.

❼ 了解同義字

_____ **2. Which word means the opposite of "aggressive"?**
(A) Friendly. (B) Beautiful. (C) Smart. (D) Proud.

❽ 了解反義字

_____ **3. In the story, "a big goose shot from the bush." What does that phrase mean?**
(A) It jumped into the bush. (B) It threw things from the bush.
(C) It hid inside the bush. (D) It ran out of the bush.

❾ 從上下文推測字義

地圖

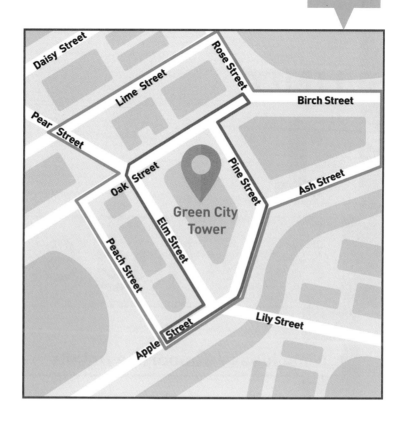

圖片

時間軸

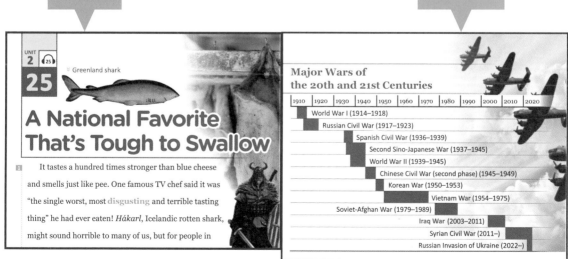

UNIT
1

Reading Skills

This unit covers six key elements you will need to focus on in order to properly understand an article: main idea(s), supporting details, making inferences, clarifying devices, author's purpose and tone, and finding bias.

In this unit, you will learn how to understand what a text is mainly about, observe how details support main ideas, make assumptions based on information in the text, identify the way a writer makes their work interesting, pinpoint the reason behind an author's writing, and discover a writer's bias.

01 A Hotel on Waves

Sail the Seven Seas in Style With Elizabeth Cruises

1   Have you ever dreamed of traveling around the world in luxury? Why not take a relaxing ocean cruise with us? Our modern cruise ships are like floating five-star hotels.

2   During your day you can take a swim in one of two large onboard swimming pools. You can also work out in the onboard gym, or watch a movie in the onboard movie theater. Our many singers, bands, and other performers will keep you entertained during the evening.

3   What's more, our top chefs will prepare three delicious meals for you each day. When you arrive at each destination, we have experienced guides to show you all the best sights and local experiences, food, and culture. So go ahead, book a cruise with us today, and get ready for the best experience of your life!

4 **Here are three amazing cruise packages to choose from.**

European Cruise	Asian Cruise	Caribbean Cruise

Length: 3 weeks	Length: 10 days	Length: 2 weeks
Price per person: HK$50,000+	Price per person: HK$25,000+	Price per person: HK$40,000+
Countries visited: Italy, France, Belgium, Portugal, Spain, Greece	Countries visited: Japan, South Korea, Singapore, Thailand, The Philippines	Places visited: Jamaica, The Bahamas, Cayman Islands, Bermuda, St. Lucia, Belize

5 **Cruises leave year-round from Hong Kong.**

Visit <u>www.elizabethcruises.com</u> for schedules and booking information.

Q UESTIONS

_____1. **What is the main idea of the ad?**
   (A) The cruise company's ships are very modern.
   (B) You will have a great time on a cruise ship.
   (C) The cruise company will provide guides to take you sightseeing.
   (D) There are three cruise packages to choose from.

_____2. **You have fourteen vacation days this year. Which cruises could you go on?**
   (A) The European Cruise or the Asian Cruise.
   (B) The European Cruise or the Caribbean Cruise.
   (C) The Caribbean Cruise or the Asian Cruise.
   (D) The Caribbean, European, or Asian Cruise.

_____3. **How much would it cost for you to take the Caribbean Cruise by yourself?**
   (A) At least HK$50,000.   (B) Between HK$25,000 and HK$40,000.
   (C) At least HK$40,000.   (D) Under HK$30,000.

_____4. **Which of these can you NOT do on one of the company's ships?**
   (A) Go swimming.   (B) Watch movies.
   (C) Listen to live music.   (D) Play soccer.

_____5. **You visit** www.elizabethcruises.com **and book a cruise.**
   Later you get the following email.

From: booking@elizabethcruises.com

Dear Customer,
      Thank you for booking the European Cruise leaving Hong Kong on Feb 1, 2023 and returning on Feb. 22, 2023.
      We have received your payment, and your booking was successful. Your booking number is 56739473. Your e-ticket should arrive soon. If you would like to make any changes to your booking, please email us at booking@elizabethcruises.com.
Best wishes,
Elizabeth Cruises

   What is the main message of this email?
   (A) You booked a three-week cruise.
   (B) Your booking was successful.
   (C) Your booking number is 56739473.
   (D) You will be leaving on February 1.

02 A Letter to My Favorite Sister

Dear Jennifer,

1 I've got something important to say. But before that, I want you to know I feel so blessed to have you as my elder sister. You're my favorite sister in the world! Remember when we went to that strawberry farm together with Mom and Dad? You showed me how to pick strawberries by pinching the stems and pulling the fruit off. It was so much more fun than shopping! Let's go there again for your birthday this year!

2 Remember my clumsy fingers? I pinched the strawberries too hard and **squirt**! The juice got on your favorite jacket. I was so worried you'd get mad at me. But when I said sorry, you just forgave me. You knew I didn't do it on purpose.

3 Jennifer, you are my superhero. You're not just kind to me, you're also kind to little animals. I know you've been helping out at the animal shelter for months now. Maybe you could bring home a kitten someday!

» strawberry farm

My dear, favorite sister, here comes the thing I do want to tell you. Last week when you were helping out at the animal shelter, I borrowed your favorite T-shirt. I accidentally got some ketchup on it. I tried to wash off the stain, but it wouldn't come off. Oops and sorry!

Love,

Chloe

⌃ helping at an animal shelter

Q UESTIONS

_____1. **Which picture best describes the main purpose of this letter?**

(A) 　(B) 　(C) 　(D)

_____2. **Which of the following is TRUE about Jennifer?**

(A) She hasn't adopted a kitten from the animal shelter.

(B) She is good at taking care of animals.

(C) She likes to eat fries with ketchup.

(D) She tries her best in everything she does.

_____3. **What is likely TRUE about Chloe?**

(A) She has never been to an animal shelter before.

(B) She wants to buy a new jacket.

(C) She asked Jennifer to teach her how to do laundry.

(D) She took Jennifer's T-shirt without asking.

_____4. **Where does Chloe say she wants to go on Jennifer's birthday this year?**

(A) A department store.　(B) A nice restaurant.

(C) The strawberry farm.　(D) The animal shelter.

_____5. **Which sentence best describes why Chloe wrote this letter?**

(A) She wants to show how much she looks up to her sister.

(B) She wants to plan her sister's birthday this year.

(C) She wants to make her sister less angry after the accident.

(D) She wants her sister to bring a kitten home from the shelter.

03 Andrés's Puppy

Tuesday, March 13

[1] When I got home from school today, Dad showed me a story from the news. It really touched me, so I wanted to write about it right away.

[2] The article said that a dog shelter in Mexico recently found a puppy outside its door. With the puppy were a soft toy and a note. The note was from a young boy named Andrés. Andrés wrote that he was leaving the dog at the shelter because his father was hurting it. He hoped that at the shelter the dog would be safe.

[3] After the shelter shared the story online, 300 people called to offer to adopt the puppy, which is great. But the shelter also reminded people that they have over 120 other dogs that need a loving home, too.

[4] The story really got me thinking. I've been asking Dad if we can get a dog for a while now. I always wanted to get one from the pet store. But after reading the story, I have changed my mind. If we do get a dog, we should get one from a shelter. There are so many dogs that have been hurt or thrown away by their previous owners and need a good home. Maybe our family can give them one.

≫ thrown-away dog

≪ dog that needs a home

Q UESTIONS

_____1. **What is the writer's main point?**
(A) The writer's father showed him a touching news story today.
(B) A dog shelter in Mexico recently found a puppy outside its doors.
(C) A news story made the writer think differently about getting a dog.
(D) The writer has been asking his father if they can get a dog for a long time.

_____2. **In the news story, what was found along with the puppy?**
(A) Some food and water.   (B) A bag of old clothes.
(C) A note and a soft toy.   (D) A picture of a boy.

_____3. **Why did Andrés's take his puppy to the shelter?**
(A) Because he did not have money to buy food for it.
(B) Because his father was hurting it.
(C) Because the dog was biting people.
(D) Because his family were going to live abroad.

⋀ dog in a shelter

_____4. **What is the main idea in the third paragraph?**
(A) The dog shelter shared their story online.
(B) Hundreds of people called to offer to adopt Andrés's puppy.
(C) There are more than 120 dogs in the dog shelter.
(D) Andrés's puppy is just one of many dogs that need a new home.

≫ adopting pets

_____5. **What has the writer been doing for a long time?**
(A) Asking his father if they can get a dog.
(B) Helping out at a dog shelter.
(C) Feeding the street dogs near his home.
(D) Sharing news stories about dogs online.

>> indoor rock climbing

04 All the Way to the Top

Kate: Hey, Jack. My family and I are going rock climbing this weekend. Do you want to join us?

Jack: Rock climbing? Hmm, I'm not sure.

Kate: Come on! It will be fun!

Jack: I've never done it before. I'm afraid I will be terrible at it.

Kate: Don't worry! There are lots of different difficulty levels. You can start on the beginners' wall and then go from there.

Jack: Maybe. I guess I should do some exercise this weekend.

Kate: Exactly! Rock climbing is a great activity. It makes your muscles stronger and it isn't stressful on your joints like some sports.

Jack: I like the sound of that. I hate feeling sore after gym class.

Kate: And it is really good for developing your coordination. It will be great for a clumsy person like you!

Jack: Ha, ha, very funny. 😛 Oh, but I have that big math test on Monday. I should probably study.

Kate: Rock climbing is good for your brain, too. It helps you develop your problem-solving abilities. So by coming with me, you will kind of be studying for your math test . . .

Jack: Well, when you put it that way . . . OK! I'll come!

Kate: Great! I'll message you the details later.

QUESTIONS

_____ 1. **What is Kate's main message to Jack?**
   (A) She and her family are going rock climbing this weekend.
   (B) He should join her and her family rock climbing this weekend.
   (C) Going rock climbing will help him prepare for his math test.
   (D) She will send him the details about rock climbing later.

easier levels

_____ 2. **Which of the following does rock climbing NOT help develop?**
   (A) Your muscles.   (B) Your coordination.
   (C) Your problem-solving abilities.   (D) Your language skills.

_____ 3. **Which of the following is TRUE about Jack?**
   (A) He goes rock climbing often.
   (B) He has never been rock climbing before.
   (C) He is very good at rock climbing.
   (D) He hates to exercise.

_____ 4. **Which of the following happens during their talk?**
   (A) Kate tells Jack where the rock climbing gym is.
   (B) Jack decides not to go rock climbing with Kate.
   (C) Kate gets angry at Jack for something he said.
   (D) Jack agrees to go rock climbing with Kate.

_____ 5. **Later that evening, Kate and Jack talk some more.**

 Kate

Jack, I'm so sorry. My dad has to work this weekend, so he can't drive us to the rock climbing gym.

 **Jack**

I see. Can we take a bus instead?

Not really. The gym isn't near a bus stop.

That's a shame. I was looking forward to going.

Me, too. Maybe we can go some other time soon.

Yes, let me know the next time you plan on going.

What is the main point of their talk this time?
   (A) The planned rock climbing trip is no longer happening.
   (B) Kate's father has to work on Saturday and Sunday.
   (C) Jack was excited for the rock climbing trip.
   (D) The rock climbing gym can only be reached by car.

05 A Letter of Advice

» being yourself

Dear Tina,

1   I just read your letter. I'm so sorry you aren't enjoying your summer camp experience. It's hard when you want to be popular but others don't seem to like you. It's also easy to think that everything will be OK if only you change your behavior to suit them.

2   You know, I was exactly the same at your age. When I was in eighth grade, I really wanted to take piano lessons. But the group I hung out with all thought that learning an instrument was uncool. So instead, I joined the soccer team with them because I wanted them to like me. I had such a miserable time that year, and I regret not learning the piano to this day.

≺ Tina is not enjoying summer camp.

» having a miserable time playing soccer

3   Can I give you some advice, mother to daughter? Don't live your life just to be liked by others. Some people are just not going to like you for who you are. (Kind of like the way you don't like my homemade chicken curry, despite the fact that it's super delicious!) You are already funny, smart, and kind. If others can't see that, then why waste your time trying to please them?

4   Remember, true happiness lies in being yourself.

All my love,
Mom

» chicken curry

QUESTIONS

_____1. **What is the writer's main point in the letter?**
 (A) She used to be part of her school's soccer team.
 (B) She thinks Tina is funny, smart, and kind.
 (C) She thinks Tina should stop trying to please others.
 (D) She feels sad that Tina is not enjoying herself.

_____2. **Where is Tina at the moment?**
 (A) At a summer camp.   (B) At school.
 (C) At home.   (D) At a friend's house.

_____3. **What is the relationship between the writer and Tina?**
 (A) They are sisters.
 (B) They are teacher and student.
 (C) They are junior high school friends.
 (D) They are mother and daughter.

_____4. **What does the writer wish she had done in eighth grade?**
 (A) Made more friends.   (B) Learned to play the piano.
 (C) Gone to a summer camp.   (D) Learned to cook chicken curry.

_____5. **What is the writer's main point in the second paragraph?**
 (A) Her friends all wanted to join the soccer team.
 (B) She wanted to please her school friends.
 (C) She understands well how Tina feels.
 (D) She did not enjoy her time in eighth grade.

06

≫ department store being cleaned

Case Number 16,563

≫ taking a virus test

1 Good evening, and welcome to the 9 o'clock news.

2 Our first story tonight: Two department stores in Tokyo have closed today after a person with COVID-19 visited them over the weekend.

3 The person, a man in his 30s with the last name **Suzuki**, took a COVID-19 test at a local hospital because he was about to go abroad on a business trip. The test came back positive even though the man did not have any symptoms.

4 Before he took the test, the man visited two department stores near where he lives. The government has already notified everyone who was there at the same time. Anyone who has received a government text message should keep an eye on their health and call their local health department if they feel ill.

5 The department stores will be closed for 24 hours while the buildings are being cleaned and all staff are being tested.

6   The source of the infection is still not known. Last month he returned from a business trip to the Philippines but tested negative at the end of his 14-day quarantine. The government is working hard to find out where he may have caught the virus.

7   The case brings Tokyo's total number of COVID-19 cases to 16,563.

8   Now, on to our main story . . .

≫ warning text message

Q UESTIONS

_____ **1. What is probably TRUE about the man with the last name Suzuki?**
- (A) He was feeling sick when he visited the department stores.
- (B) He did not tell the government that he visited the department stores.
- (C) He will have to give the department stores money because they had to close.
- (D) He did not know he had COVID-19 when he visited the department stores.

_____ **2. Which of the following must be TRUE?**
- (A) All staff in the department stores will go into 14-day quarantine.
- (B) The man is for now the latest COVID-19 case in Tokyo.
- (C) Government officials don't think he gave COVID-19 to anyone.
- (D) The man will still be able to go on his business trip.

_____ **3. What can we infer about the man's travel habits?**
- (A) He travels abroad often for business.
- (B) He doesn't like traveling alone.
- (C) He does not have enough money to travel often.
- (D) He prefers to travel by sea than by air.

_____ **4. What is the news mostly made up of?**
- (A) Opinions.   (B) Guesses.   (C) Facts.   (D) Wishes.

_____ **5. What does the speaker do at the end of the fourth paragraph?**
- (A) Give a piece of advice.   (B) Explain what's happening.
- (C) Give a surprising number.   (D) Make a guess about the future.

» studio apartment with
a large window

Looking for
a New Place

1 **Bright studio apartment ready to rent now
in London—just £350 a week!**

2 Big enough for one person. The room has its own bathroom
—no need to share with others! Desk, chair, large bed, closet,
washing machine, and fridge are all provided. The room also
has a large window that lets in lots of light. And there is a small
balcony with a table and chair.

3 Good location, near University College London. The area is lively
and has many stores and cafés. The place is a five-minute walk
from the Tube station. There are several bike sharing stations
close by, too. For food, there is a supermarket nearby, along with
many restaurants and several convenience stores.

4 No cats or dogs are allowed, but pets such as fish, turtles, and
other quiet, small animals are fine. Must rent for at least one
year. Must pay the first month's rent up front, plus a security
deposit (one month's rent × 2). Electricity and water bills are not
included in the rent.

5 Call me (**James, the landlord**) if you want to check out the place.
I am free during the evenings 6 p.m. to 9 p.m., Monday to Friday, and
9 a.m. to 9 p.m. on weekends. Looking forward to your call!

⌄ having one's own bathroom

⌄ Tube station and supermarket

Q UESTIONS

_____1. **What can we guess about** James, the landlord?
(A) He thinks people are usually careful using water and electricity.
(B) He thinks £350 a week rent is expensive.
(C) He thinks most people don't like dark apartments.
(D) He thinks most people who will apply will own their own car.

_____2. **Why doesn't the landlord want cats and dogs in this apartment?**
(A) They make too much noise.
(B) They are too expensive.
(C) They need lots of exercise.
(D) They make some people sick.

_____3. **Which of the following people is the apartment a good fit for?**
(A) A large family of four.
(B) Someone who likes to live around quiet places.
(C) A fun-loving college student.
(D) Someone who is visiting London for a few months.

_____4. **What does the writer provide in the fourth paragraph?**
(A) Some suggestions. (B) Some rules.
(C) Some problems. (D) Some jokes.

_____5. **Someone left the landlord a message.**

> Hi James, my name is Evan. I saw your ad online. What a great apartment! I would love to come and take a look tonight at 7 p.m. Also, is £350 the cheapest you will go? **How about** if I sign for two years instead of one. Can you make it a little cheaper then? If that's fine with you, please send me the address so I can come by and check it out.

What does "How about" here show?
(A) That Evan is going to give an example.
(B) That Evan is going to refuse something.
(C) That Evan is going to accept something.
(D) That Evan is going to suggest something.

» family meal

08 A Long and Happy Life

In Memory of
June Smith
January 23, 1935 – March 12, 2022

1 After a long and happy life, June Smith passed away peacefully on March 12, 2022, aged 87. She is survived by her two sons, Joseph and Mark, her daughter, Sally, and seven grandchildren.

2 June was born in Greentown in 1935. As a girl, she loved nature and spent many hours outdoors climbing trees and collecting flowers. As an adult, she joined the Greentown Parks Department. She spent her life working hard to make sure Greentown had many natural spaces for everyone to enjoy. It was at the Parks Department that she met **Rob**, who later became her loving husband.

3 June loved her family deeply. Her favorite times of year were holidays, when her children and grandchildren would come home and celebrate together. She took enormous pleasure in cooking for the whole family, and her delicious meals will be sorely missed by all who tasted her wonderful cooking. Most of all, she enjoyed spending time with her grandchildren, teaching them to cook and showing them love.

4 A funeral will be held for June at the Adam's Street Church on Thursday, March 24, 2022 at 1 p.m. All who knew and loved her are welcome to join the family in celebrating her life.

≫ funeral

QUESTIONS

_____1. **What can we guess about June Smith?**
   (A) She died in a car accident.   (B) She was a caring person.
   (C) She enjoyed traveling the world.   (D) She was good at math.

_____2. **What can we guess about June's husband Rob?**
   (A) He still works for the Greentown Parks Department.
   (B) He was married once before.
   (C) He did not like June's cooking.
   (D) He died before June.

_____3. **How does the writer organize the information in the second paragraph?**
   (A) From earliest to latest.
   (B) From latest to earliest.
   (C) From least important to most important.
   (D) From most important to least important.

_____4. **How does the writer end the article?**
   (A) With a problem.   (B) With a joke.
   (C) With an invitation.   (D) With a wish.

_____5. **Which of these most likely shows what June would be doing during the holidays?**

(A)    (B)

(C)    (D)

09

» The clouds are below you.

The Climb

1
One step at a time, that's how I'll do it.

Just one foot after the other.

I'll tell myself over and over again:

The mountain makes me stronger.

2
Far ahead of me, my brother shouts:

"Can it really be much farther?"

Four thousand five hundred thirty-three meters tall!

The mountain makes me stronger.

3
Seeing me struggle, my father asks:

"Think you can go on much longer?"

"Don't worry about me," I say. "I'll keep on going."

The mountain makes me stronger.

QUESTIONS

_____1. **What form does the reading take?**

    (A) A play.   (B) A diary entry.

    (C) A poem.   (D) A conversation.

_____2. **What does the writer do in the first paragraph?**

    (A) Offer a review.   (B) Tell a joke.

    (C) Give an example.   (D) Explain a plan.

_____3. **How is the writer feeling in the fourth paragraph?**

    (A) Tired.   (B) Hungry.

    (C) Lonely.   (D) Worried.

≫ one foot after the other

≫ closed for bad weather

4　　My head spins, my legs feel like stone,

But step by step I conquer.

When I reach the top, I'll feel as light as air!

The mountain makes me stronger.

5　　After a while I look up from my feet.

Below me, are those clouds? I wonder.

Have I really made it all this way?

The mountain makes me stronger.

6　"I'm sorry," a man says, "you'll have to turn back.

The summit is closed for bad weather."

My brother cries like it's the end of the world,

But not me.

The mountain has made me stronger.

_____ **4. The writer of the poem is from Switzerland. Look at the list of Switzerland's tallest mountains on the right. Which of them did the writer most likely climb?**

(A) Monte Rosa　　　　(B) Dom

(C) Lyskamm　　　　　(D) Weisshorn

_____ **5. What can we guess about the writer's trip?**

(A) It made the writer hate mountain climbing.

(B) It changed the writer for the better.

(C) It changed the writer's opinion of his father.

(D) It made the writer want to be a teacher.

Mountain Name
(Height)

❶ Monte Rosa
(4,634 m)

❷ Dom
(4,545 m)

❸ Lyskamm
(4,533 m)

❹ Weisshorn
(4,506 m)

(Source: Wikipedia)

10 The Highest Form of Art There Is

⌃ portraits of the famous rulers Elizabeth I and Wu Zetian

⌃ *The Weeping Woman* (1937)
(cc by NichoDesign)

⌃ *Mona Lisa* (1503–1506)

1 Da Vinci's *Mona Lisa*, Picasso's *The Weeping Woman*, Edvard Munch's *The Scream*: Each of these great works of art is painted in a unique style. But they do have something in common. They are all portraits.

2 Portraits are a very important part of art history. Think about life before photos were invented. One of the few ways to capture one's own image was through painting. Ancient rulers would get artists to paint their portraits in order to inspire awe in their subjects and keep their memory alive long after death. Later, it became common for middle-class people to pay for portraits of themselves and their loved ones, too. In fact, for a long time, painting portraits was one of the best ways artists could make money.

3 Looking deeply at a portrait can be an amazing experience. The clothes people are wearing and objects they are holding all tell us something about their

» Van Gogh's self-portrait (1889)

personalities and time. What's more, many famous painters, such as Munch, Vincent van Gogh, and Frida Kahlo, opened their souls to the world by painting themselves. Indeed, portraits are a meeting point between psychology and history. This is why for me and many other art lovers, portrait painting is the highest form of art there is.

≈ *The Scream* (1893)

Q UESTIONS

_____1. **How does the writer start the article?**
    (A) With some examples.   (B) With a joke.
    (C) With a difficult question.   (D) With a surprising number.

_____2. **How does the writer create interest in the second paragraph?**
    (A) By asking the reader to imagine the future.
    (B) By asking the reader to imagine they were someone else.
    (C) By asking the reader to imagine the past.
    (D) By asking the reader to imagine they lived in a different country.

_____3. **Which of the following most likely happened after photos were invented?**
    (A) Artists almost totally stopped painting portraits of other people.
    (B) More poor families began asking for painted portraits.
    (C) Artists could no longer count on painting portraits to make money.
    (D) Artists made more money painting portraits than ever before.

_____4. **Which of the following is likely TRUE?**
    (A) The writer of the passage is an artist.
    (B) The writer enjoys looking at portraits.
    (C) The writer has never seen a portrait.
    (D) The writer's favorite artist is Frida Kahlo.

_____5. **How does the writer end the passage?**
    (A) With a wish.   (B) With a new idea.
    (C) With a true story.   (D) With a personal thought.

11 Goodbye Junior High

1 My fellow students, can you believe that it's been three years already? Just a short time ago we were just silly little kids. Now we are ready for high school!

2 I won't lie: When I arrived here, I was scared. The older kids scared me. **Principal Jackson** *really* scared me! But I soon discovered how kind everyone was, and soon I felt right at home.

3 Our amazing teachers have all worked so hard to give us a good education. They are real heroes. High school will be tough, but our teachers have prepared us well. They have taught us not only their subjects but also how to work hard and never quit. I feel I've learned so much here that my head might explode, just like one of **Mr. Wang**'s crazy science experiments!

4 Many of us will be going to different high schools. We will no longer be together every day. This makes me very sad. But we should also be happy for all the great friends we have made here. No matter where you go from here, know that your junior high school friends will always be there to support you.

5 Thank you, and good luck to everyone for the future!

» graduation

>> science experiments

Q UESTIONS

_____ 1. **Which of these does the speaker clearly have strong, good feelings for?**
(A) The school principal.   (B) His teachers.
(C) His old school.   (D) His future high school.

_____ 2. **Why does the speaker mention Mr. Wang's science experiments?**
(A) To make the listeners sad.
(B) To make the listeners excited.
(C) To make the listeners angry.
(D) To make the listeners laugh.

_____ 3. **What is the speaker's tone in the fourth paragraph?**
(A) Cheerful.   (B) Worried.
(C) Surprised.   (D) Mean.

_____ 4. **Which of the following is a biased sentence?**
(A) We will no longer be together every day.
(B) Many of us will be going to different high schools.
(C) Just a short time ago we were just silly little kids.
(D) Now we are ready for high school!

_____ 5. **Below is a note from Principal Jackson to the speaker. What is the purpose of the note?**

> Dear Kim,
>
> Just a quick note to say how much I appreciated your kind words about our school. I am so glad you had such a happy time here, even though I scared you on your first day! Best of luck to you in high school. I know you will make your new school proud just like you have made us proud.
>
> Best wishes,
> Principal Jackson

(A) To scare the speaker.   (B) To thank the speaker.
(C) To teach the speaker.   (D) To invite the speaker.

>> dung beetle (cc by division, CSIRO)

12 Nature's Little Helpers

➡ Nature's Little Helpers

1 Each month we take a look at an **amazing** creature that helps out other plants and animals. This time we can't wait to tell you about the tiny but very important dung beetle!

⌃ breaking out of the nest

2 Dung beetles are insects that collect animal dung and use it for food and nesting. When a dung beetle comes across a nice, **fresh** piece of dung, it digs a hole in the earth and takes it safely below ground. A female will then lay her eggs on it, and when the eggs hatch, the babies feed on the delicious dung until they are grown.

3 Some people might think dung beetles are disgusting, but those people are just **ignorant**. In fact, the beetles' behavior is very helpful to both plants and animals alike. By taking the dung below ground, dung beetles help mix

>> dung beetle carrying a ball of dung

⌃ baby dung beetle feeding on dung

⚠ The activity of dung beetles is wonderful for plants.

⚠ Dung beetles help keep the earth nutritious for plants.

it with the earth. This keeps the earth full of nutrients, which is wonderful for plants. Moreover, burying the dung stops flies from laying their eggs in it. This means there will be fewer of these nasty bugs to spread diseases and bother **poor** animals like cows.

4

 Next time: We'll tell you how elephants help other animals find water to drink during the dry season.

Q UESTIONS

_____1. **What is the purpose of this magazine article?**
   (A) To teach the reader something interesting.
   (B) To give the reader an answer to a difficult question.
   (C) To show the reader how to do something.
   (D) To sell the reader something useful.

_____2. **Which of the following is NOT a biased word in the article?**
   (A) Amazing.　(B) Ignorant.　(C) Poor.　(D) Fresh.

_____3. **Which type of creature mentioned in the article does the writer show bias against?**
   (A) Cows.　(B) Elephants.　(C) Flies.　(D) Dung beetles.

_____4. **What is the writer's purpose in the final sentence of the article?**
   (Next time: We'll tell . . . during the dry season.)
   (A) To make you want to read the next page of the magazine.
   (B) To make you look forward to next month's magazine.
   (C) To make you feel worried about something bad.
   (D) To make you think differently about elephants.

_____5. **What is the writer's tone in the first paragraph?**
   (A) Excited.　(B) Angry.　(C) Sad.　(D) Scared.

13 Sweden's Saturday Candy

Prof. Brown's Tooth Health Blog

November 7, 2023 | by Prof. Brown

1 These days so many kids have mouths full of black teeth, and as a dentist, I feel my blood boil when I see them! Why do those careless parents let their kids eat mountains of candy every single day?

2 Last month, I was invited to Sweden to give a talk, and something surprised me: All the kids I saw seemed to have great teeth. And yet, on Saturday, the candy stores were full of people. How were these children eating so many sweets but still maintaining healthy teeth? I asked a Swedish colleague to explain, and he said it was due to a Swedish **tradition** called *lördagsgodis*—"Saturday candy."

3 According to my colleague, the tradition started in the 1950s. Sweden was getting **richer**, and the government was afraid this would result in kids eating lots of sugar. So the government suggested that parents make candy a once-a-week treat. Many parents tried it, and it was successful. Today, it has become a fun part of Swedish **culture**. Kids look

« Swedish sweets

⌃ Swedish candy store

forward all week to going candy shopping on Saturday, and they don't ruin their teeth by eating candy seven days a week.

4   We could really learn a lesson from those **intelligent** Swedes. I really hope this idea can take off around the world someday, too.

Q UESTIONS

_____1. **What is the writer's tone in the first paragraph?**
(A) Loving.   (B) Bored.   (C) Excited.   (D) Angry.

_____2. **What is the writer's main purpose in writing the post?**
(A) To make people want to buy more candy.
(B) To make people want to travel to Sweden.
(C) To show a better way for kids to enjoy candy.
(D) To teach people about Swedish culture.

_____3. **Who does the writer show bias against?**
(A) Today's parents.   (B) Today's dentists.
(C) His Swedish colleague.   (D) The Swedish government.

_____4. **Which of the following is a biased word in the blog post?**
(A) Richer.   (B) Intelligent.   (C) Tradition.   (D) Culture.

_____5. **On what tone does the writer end the post?**
(A) A funny one.   (B) A sorry one.
(C) A thankful one.   (D) A wishful one.

14 Making Up After Falling Out

1 Emily: Hello, everyone. Welcome to our show. Sometimes, friends argue. This is a normal part of friendships, but how do we overcome conflicts when we have them? Luckily, we have Dr. Mary here to help us with some suggestions.

2 Dr. Mary: To deal with conflicts, we really need to calm down. It's impossible to resolve a conflict when we are feeling angry. Secondly, we must talk to the other person face to face. It's easy for you or your friend to get the wrong information if you get it from someone else, and that could make things worse.

3 It's also very important to listen to the other person. There are two sides to every story! Next, we need to use *I* statements when we talk to let the other person know how we feel. For example, "I feel angry when you don't answer my calls." It tells the other person exactly how you are feeling.

4 Don't forget to apologize if you are to blame. Many people don't feel comfortable saying sorry, but it shows we understand we were wrong. Finally, we need to come together to find a solution to the conflict that makes both friends feel good. This is the most important part!

5 Emily: Those are great ideas. Thank you!

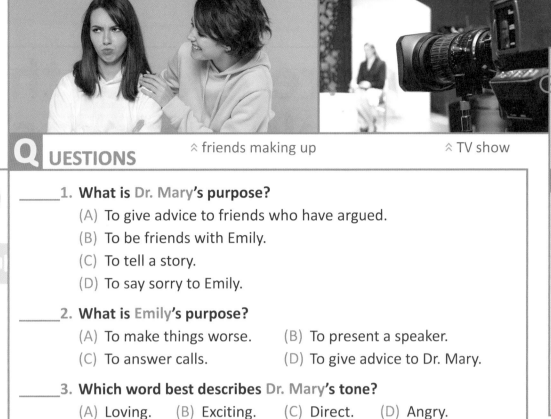

⊼ friends making up

⊼ TV show

UNIT 1 Reading Skills 1-3 Author's Purpose & Tone / Finding Bias

Q UESTIONS

_____1. **What is Dr. Mary's purpose?**
   (A) To give advice to friends who have argued.
   (B) To be friends with Emily.
   (C) To tell a story.
   (D) To say sorry to Emily.

_____2. **What is Emily's purpose?**
   (A) To make things worse.   (B) To present a speaker.
   (C) To answer calls.   (D) To give advice to Dr. Mary.

_____3. **Which word best describes Dr. Mary's tone?**
   (A) Loving.   (B) Exciting.   (C) Direct.   (D) Angry.

_____4. **Below is an email Sophie sent to her friend.**

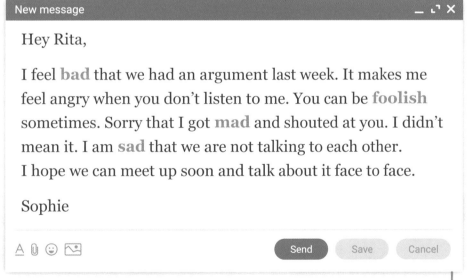

New message   _ ⌐⌐ ✕

Hey Rita,

I feel **bad** that we had an argument last week. It makes me
feel angry when you don't listen to me. You can be **foolish**
sometimes. Sorry that I got **mad** and shouted at you. I didn't
mean it. I am **sad** that we are not talking to each other.
I hope we can meet up soon and talk about it face to face.

Sophie

A ⎁ ☺ ⊠   Send   Save   Cancel

What is Sophie's purpose?
   (A) To argue with Rita.   (B) To make Rita feel bad.
   (C) To tell Rita she is mean. (D) To resolve a conflict with Rita.

_____5. **Which of the following words from the email above is a biased word?**
   (A) Bad.   (B) Mad.   (C) Foolish.   (D) Sad.

15 Where Are All the Female Coaches?

1 When you picture the coach of a successful sports team, do you see a man or a woman? Most of you probably picture a man, but why? We know that men aren't always better teachers, and there are lots of great female **leaders** in both politics and business. Why, then, are there so few women leading sports teams? In the United States, for example, 60% of women's college sports teams are coached by men, while only 3% of male teams are coached by women! This is a **crazy** situation and has to change.

2 Indeed, anyone who thinks women can't coach as well as men needs to think more clearly. Ever heard of **Pat Summitt**? She won a silver medal at Olympic basketball and then went on to become one of the best coaches in United States college basketball **history**. She led her team to over a thousand wins, more than any other coach in college basketball history at the time. Cutting out great coaches just because they are women really is

» female coach and her team

« Pat Summitt receives the Presidential Medal of Freedom at the White House.

just so stupid. Think how many more games a team could win if they employed a skillful, **experienced** female coach instead of an average male one.

3   In short, sports managers need to think very hard about their own biases when it comes to choosing a new coach. By ignoring women, they really are shooting themselves in the foot.

Q UESTIONS

_____ 1. **What is the writer's tone in the first paragraph?**

(A) Joking.   (B) Scared.   (C) Confused.   (D) Cruel.

_____ 2. **Why does the writer mention Pat Summitt?**

(A) To show that sports managers often ignore female coaches.

(B) To show that men are better coaches than women.

(C) To show that women can make great political or business leaders.

(D) To show that women can be as good at coaching as men.

_____ 3. **Which of the following is a biased word in the passage?**

(A) Leader.   (B) Crazy.   (C) History.   (D) Experienced.

_____ 4. **Which of the following is NOT a biased sentence?**

(A) Indeed, anyone who thinks women can't coach as well as men needs to think more clearly.

(B) In the United States, for example, 60% of women's college sports teams are coached by men.

(C) By ignoring women, they really are shooting themselves in the foot.

(D) Cutting out great coaches just because they are women really is just so stupid.

_____ 5. **What is the writer's tone in the final paragraph?**

(A) Certain.   (B) Friendly.   (C) Nervous.   (D) Shy.

Let's Talk About Fish!

1 *In Teacher Mike's class, the students are having a discussion.*

2 **Maggie:** I think aquariums are great. You can see lots of **different** kinds of **colorful** fish up close at one time. I love visiting the city aquarium with my parents. We always have a good time. They also allow scientists to study fish more easily.

3 **Peter:** I don't agree. In the ocean fish can swim around freely. I think it's **cruel** to keep them in a small area. I also think being around so many people is stressful for them. Fish have feelings, too.

4 **Luke:** Maybe, but the ocean is a dangerous place. At least in an aquarium, the fish are safe. I agree with Maggie. I think it's great that we can get so close to nature even though we live in a **big** city. Aquariums let city people learn about sea life firsthand.

5 **Laura:** I'm more worried about the care fish get at aquariums. What if the people who work there don't do a good job? I think it's better to leave fish in the ocean, where they naturally belong.

6 **Teacher Mike:** I think you all gave very good points for and against. Let's put this to a class vote. Hands up everyone who thinks aquariums are a good idea.

⌄ The ocean can be
a dangerous place.

#

Q UESTIONS

_____1. **What is the purpose of the discussion?**
   (A) To decide where to go for a class trip.
   (B) To hear Luke's opinions on life in a city.
   (C) To decide whether aquariums are a good idea.
   (D) To learn about different kinds of fish.

_____2. **What is Peter's main point?**
   (A) Fish have feelings, too.
   (B) Fish do not have enough space in an aquarium.
   (C) He doesn't agree with Maggie.
   (D) It's stressful to be in a crowd of people.

_____3. **What is TRUE about Maggie?**
   (A) Her parents often take her to an aquarium.
   (B) She is the oldest in the class.
   (C) Her father works in a pet store.
   (D) She is scared of fish.

_____4. **Which of the following is a biased word?**
   (A) Colorful.   (B) Big.   (C) Cruel.   (D) Different.

_____5. **At the end of the discussion, Teacher Mike took a vote. He made a chart of the result. Here it is. Whose ideas were the most popular?**

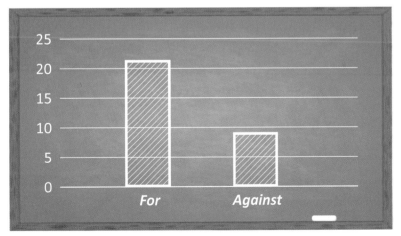

⌃ staff member in
an aquarium

   (A) Maggie's and Laura's.   (B) Maggie's and Luke's.
   (C) Laura's and Peter's.   (D) Peter's and Luke's.

» social distancing

17 New Rules for Our Restaurant

1 *Julia, a restaurant manager, is hosting an emergency staff meeting.*

2   Good morning, everyone. Thank you for coming in early today for this meeting. We have several important items to discuss today. You each should have a **list** of them in front of you.

3   The first thing I have to tell you about is our new shorter business hours. Due to the recent rise in cases of COVID-19, the government has told all restaurants that they need to restrict their business hours. Usually we open from 11:30 a.m. to 9 p.m., Tuesday to Sunday. But starting from next week, we will only be opening for dinner—5 p.m. to 9 p.m.—and we will be cutting our weekend service altogether. These new rules will last for at least six weeks.

4   I know this means a lot of you will lose work hours and pay. But please don't worry too much. The government has said that it will provide you with any lost pay during this time. I will give you the necessary paperwork and show you how you apply for that later in the meeting.

5   OK, **next** we need to discuss rearranging our tables and chairs so that they allow social distancing . . .

Q UESTIONS

_____ 1. **What is the main idea of the article?**
    (A) The restaurant needs to change its business hours because of COVID-19.
    (B) The restaurant is usually closed on Mondays but open the rest of the week.
    (C) The restaurant's new business hours will last for at least six weeks.
    (D) The restaurant will no longer be opening on weekends.

_____ 2. **What will the restaurant's opening times be starting from next week?**
    (A) Tuesday to Sunday, 11:30 a.m. to 9 p.m.
    (B) Monday to Sunday, 5 p.m. to 9 p.m.
    (C) Tuesday to Friday, 11:30 a.m. to 9 p.m.
    (D) Tuesday to Friday, 5 p.m. to 9 p.m.

_____ 3. **Which of these is probably the list that Julia mentions at the start of the meeting?**

(A)
Spaghetti and meatballs
Hamburger and fries
Steak and vegetables
Ice cream
Chocolate cake
Coffee or tea

(B)
Julia, Manager
Tina, Waitress
Tom, Waiter
Mary, Cook,
Matt, Kitchen helper
Danny, Dishwasher

(C)
Monday, closed
Tuesday, dinner only
Wednesday, dinner only
Thursday, dinner only
Friday, dinner only
Weekend, closed

(D)
Welcome
New business hours
Rearranging tables and chairs
New rules for mask wearing
Applying for lost pay
Closing words

_____ 4. **What is Julia the manager's tone in the fourth paragraph?**
    (A) Angry.   (B) Caring.   (C) Excited.   (D) Bored.

_____ 5. **What does the word "next" in the final sentence show?**
    (A) Where something should be put.
    (B) The order in which something happened.
    (C) That a new topic will follow.
    (D) That a new action will follow.

18 Lost Dog!

Lost Dog!
Please help find Charlie!

1   Our dog **Charlie** went missing on August 20 and we haven't seen him since. He ran away while we were walking him in the Central Forest Park and he may still be in that area. He had a brown collar on when he disappeared. Please help us find Charlie!

2   ⚠   Charlie is a large, mixed-breed dog. His hair is mostly yellow, but he has white spots all over his body, including the tip of his tail. He weighs around 40 kilograms and is around 50 centimeters tall.

3   ⚠   He likes treats and enjoys playing with his toys. He is very friendly and he will come to you if you call his name. He loves meeting new people. He can get quite excited when he wants to play.

⌃ dog treats

⌃ dog toys

4 ⚠ Whoever finds him will receive $200 reward.

5 ⚠ Please call **(432) 123-1234** or send us a message through our Twitter account @joydog123 at any time if you see him or even think it might be him.

6 We are very worried as Charlie is not used to being away from his family, and we want him home as soon as possible.

Q UESTIONS

_____1. **What is the main idea of this reading?**
   (A) Some people have a dog called Charlie.
   (B) Some people are trying to find their missing dog.
   (C) There are many different breeds of dogs.
   (D) Dogs like to run in the Central Forest Park.

_____2. **What is the writer's purpose in this reading?**
   (A) To find their dog.
   (B) To give back a dog they has found.
   (C) To find their way out of the park.
   (D) To tell others about their dog.

_____3. **What is the writer's tone?**
   (A) Sad.　　(B) Happy.　　(C) Worried.　　(D) Angry.

_____4. **Which of these is probably TRUE about Charlie?**
   (A) He is afraid of people.　(B) He likes to run away from his family.
   (C) He is a dangerous dog.　(D) He enjoys playing games.

_____5. **How does the writer describe Charlie to the reader?**
   (A) By using a list of facts.　(B) By using a joke.
   (C) By using a strange story.　(D) By comparing him to another dog.

» When you see someone unconscious, the first step is to tap the person and call an ambulance.

19 6 Steps to Save a Life

1 You find someone unconscious on the floor. What do you do?

Here are six simple steps that you can take to help save that person's life.

2 Step 1. Call an ambulance

Tap the person gently and ask if he/she is OK.

If he/she doesn't wake up, call an ambulance right away.

3 Step 2. Turn the person onto their back

Carefully, turn the person onto his/her back.

Tilt his/her head back and open his/her mouth.

Look inside. If there is anything there, remove it.

⌃ tilting one's head

Q UESTIONS

_____1. **What is the writer's purpose in writing the article?**
   (A) To teach the reader something useful.
   (B) To help the reader change a bad habit.
   (C) To make the reader care about a topic.
   (D) To make the reader excited about an event.

_____2. **What is the main idea of the reading?**
   (A) When you perform chest presses, you should always place one hand on top of the other.
   (B) If you find someone unconscious, you can save his/her life by following a few easy steps.
   (C) If an unconscious person is breathing, you do not have to perform chest presses.
   (D) The first thing you should do when you find an unconscious person is call an ambulance.

4 ## Step 3. Check for breathing

Lower your ear to the person's mouth and listen. If he/she is breathing, just wait until the ambulance arrives. If you hear nothing after 10 seconds, proceed to the next steps.

5 ## Step 4. Perform 30 chest presses

Place one of your hands on top of the other and keep them together. Press hard and fast in the middle of the person's chest. Count until you have done 30 of these presses.

6 ## Step 5. Perform two breaths

Tilt the person's head back, hold his/her nose, and open his/her mouth. **Then** place your mouth over his/hers and breathe out. His/her chest should rise and fall. Do this twice.

7 ## Step 6. Repeat

Repeat steps 4 and 5 until the person starts to breathe or the ambulance arrives.

_____3. **For how long should you check to see if someone unconscious is breathing?**
   (A) Thirty seconds.   (B) Two seconds.
   (C) Ten seconds.   (D) One minute.

_____4. **Which of these is likely TRUE based on the article?**
   (A) You should not perform these steps if you are a girl.
   (B) If the person wakes up, you should keep preforming chest presses.
   (C) Steps 4 and 5 might not work the first time.
   (D) Step 5 will only work if you exercise a lot.

_____5. **What does the word "then" in step 5 show?**
   (A) The time that something happened.
   (B) The order in which something happened.
   (C) That a result will follow.
   (D) That a new action will follow.

20 Video Messages for Laura

*Below are some video messages made for **Laura**.*

Meggy: Laura, we have been friends since first grade. Now you're going to a new school in a new country. I hope you have a wonderful adventure there, but please don't forget me! Remember, you can call or message me anytime! Good luck in France!

Mr. Smith: I know moving to another country can be frightening. But you are a very smart and brave young woman. I know you will adapt to the new language and customs quickly. The other teachers and I all wish you well. We hope you'll come back and visit us and tell us lots of amazing stories about your new life!

Aunt Amy: When your father told me he was taking his family to France I was furious! Now I won't get to see my favorite niece every weekend! But he's promised I can come and visit you soon. We can visit all the art museums together! I can't wait!

Sarah: You're leaving forever! Whose homework will I copy when you're gone? But seriously, school is going to be terrible without you, my friend. I made you this gift, so you don't get cold and you'll remember me whenever you wear it. Send me your address, and I'll mail it to you!

Q UESTIONS

_____1. **What is happening to Laura?**
   (A) She is going on vacation.
   (B) She is getting a new job.
   (C) She is going to college.
   (D) She is moving to another country.

_____2. **What is the main idea in Meggy's video?**
   (A) Meggy wants to stay friends with Laura.
   (B) Meggy thinks Laura will have a good time.
   (C) Meggy and Laura have been friends for a long time.
   (D) Laura can call Meggy if she wants to.

_____3. **How does Mr. Smith begin his speech?**
   (A) By showing understanding.
   (B) By giving an answer to a problem.
   (C) By making a joke.
   (D) By giving an example.

_____4. **How does the tone change in Aunt Amy's video?**
   (A) From happy to sad.
   (B) From frightened to calm.
   (C) From funny to serious.
   (D) From angry to excited.

_____5. **Which of these is most likely the gift that Sarah made for Laura?**

(A)

(B)

(C)

(D)

UNIT
2

Word Study

In this unit, you will practice identifying words with the same or opposite meanings, and guessing the meanings of words from their context. These skills will help you understand new vocabulary and build vocabulary on your own in the future.

21 A Question From "Confused"

Ask Anne

Every month, Anne Smith answers your difficult questions . . .

Question 1

Dear Anne,

I have a problem. Some of my friends are starting to talk about dating. They often want to **chat** with each other about the boys they like. But I don't really want to date anyone right now. I am just in junior high school. I think there will be lots of time for dating later. Right now, I just want to have fun with my friends. But I'm afraid that if I don't pretend to be interested in dating, they will think I'm strange and **make fun of** me. What should I do?

Confused

Q UESTIONS

_____ 1. **Which of these is another word for "chat"?**

(A) Date. (B) Talk. (C) Start. (D) Think.

_____ 2. **What does "make fun of" most likely mean?**

(A) Play with. (B) Care about. (C) Laugh at. (D) Give away.

_____ 3. **What does Anne mean by "that kind of thing"?**

(A) Dating. (B) Having fun.

(C) Asking for help. (D) Being honest.

_____ 4. **What is another word for "hobbies"?**

(A) Lessons. (B) Interests. (C) Friends. (D) Teachers.

» having trouble
with friends

⌃ focusing on hobbies

Anne says:

Dear Confused,

You are not alone. This is a common problem for many young people.
Some get interested in dating before others. But there's nothing
strange about not wanting to take part in **that kind of thing** yet.
In fact, I think it's good that you aren't thinking about dating at your
age. It allows you to focus on other things, like your education, your
family, and your **hobbies**. You're right. There will be plenty of time
for it later. Just be honest with your friends about how you feel.
If they are good friends, then they won't give you any trouble.

Anne

_____5. **"Confused" wrote a second email to Anne. Read it and answer the question.**

To: **Ask Anne**

Subject: **No Longer Confused!**

Dear Anne,

Thank you for your advice. It was very **helpful**. I did what you said and my
friends were very understanding. We still talk about dating sometimes, but
I don't feel any pressure to take part any more. Keep up the great work!

(No longer) Confused

Which of these is the opposite of "helpful"?

(A) Kind.　　　(B) Friendly.　　　(C) Difficult.　　　(D) Useless.

22 Yoga for Students: Two Poses to Improve Your Memory

1   An exam is coming up. You are burning the midnight oil. You've gone through all your notes, but for some reason, you can't remember what you just read. Does this sound like you? Many students want to know: How do I improve my memory before an exam? The answer: Yoga!

2   Practicing yoga can be good for your health and mind. Studies have shown that when you practice yoga, your brain receives more oxygen. This boosts your memory and helps you to remember things more clearly.

3   When you practice yoga, your body also releases chemicals called *endorphins*, which can improve your focus. You'll be able to recall more of the notes you've studied. Also, they help you feel good and learn better!

4   Please see the next page for two poses that can boost your memory.

Q UESTIONS

_____ 1. **Which of the following shows someone who is "burning the midnight oil"?**

(A)

(B)

(C)

(D)

« practicing
yoga

Fish pose

To do this pose:

❶ Lie down on the ground and face up.

❷ Bring your arms to your sides.

❸ Use your forearms to help lift your chest.

❹ Drop your head back. Rest your head on the mat.

❺ Keep your legs and feet on the ground.

Hero pose

To do this pose:

❶ Kneel on the floor with your knees touching and your feet apart.

❷ Sit back between your feet.

❸ Keep your back straight.

❹ Bring your hands together in front of your chest.

_____ 2. **Which of the following is the opposite of "boost"?**

(A) Lower.　　(B) Improve.　　(C) Notice.　　(D) Check.

_____ 3. **What does the word "releases" mean in the reading?**

(A) Holds onto.　(B) Enjoys.　　(C) Owns.　　(D) Lets out.

_____ 4. **Which of the following has the same meaning as "recall" in the third paragraph?**

(A) Study.　　(B) Practice.　　(C) Answer.　　(D) Remember.

_____ 5. **What does "straight" mean in the reading?**

(A) Direct.　　(B) Not bent.　　(C) Honest.　　(D) Not lying.

23 Exercise Bike for Sale!

For Sale: Second-Hand Exercise Bike

- Model: Superfit 3000
- Made in Germany
- Used but **in very good condition**
- Can **deliver** anywhere in the Boston area.

Price: **$249.99**
(or best offer) »

Question 1

Mike_C:
Hi, this looks great. It might be a bit too big for my apartment, though. What are the bike's measurements?

Answer:
The bike is 1.5 m long and 50 cm wide.

Question 2

Diane_M:
Can I ask how heavy it is? I'm afraid I won't be able to carry it up the stairs in my building.

Answer:
It's 30 kg. It should be fine to carry. But if you need help, I can help you carry it upstairs when I deliver it to you.

≫ sensitivity to noise

≪ screen

Question 3

Kiki_W:
I have elderly neighbors who are very sensitive to noise. Does the bike make a lot of sound when you use it?

Answer:
No, not at all. In fact, it's almost silent.

Question 4

Xiao_K:
I see there's an LED screen at the front of the bike. What information does it show?

Answer:
The screen shows distance, speed, time spent exercising, and the number of calories you have burned.

Read More... »

Q UESTIONS

____1. **What does the phrase "in very good condition" most likely mean?**
   (A) Used by many people.   (B) Very expensive.
   (C) Easy to use.   (D) Almost like new.

____2. **Which of these words is the opposite of "deliver"?**
   (A) Pick up.   (B) Put down.   (C) Go away.   (D) Break in.

____3. **What does the word "burned" mean in the passage?**
   (A) Hurt.   (B) Cooked.   (C) Used.   (D) Found.

____4. **What word in the passage is another word for "living space"?**
   (A) Apartment.   (B) Stairs.   (C) Screen.   (D) Distance.

____5. **Which word in the passage means "totally quiet"?**
   (A) Second-hand.   (B) Silent.   (C) Wide.   (D) Elderly.

24 Bring More Books Into Your Life!

1 Studies have shown that reading often is great for your imagination, your memory, and your mental health. But if you aren't someone who naturally picks up a book when bored, forming a **regular** reading habit can be hard. If you'd like to read more, here are a few things you can try.

2 First, always carry a book with you. When you leave the house in the morning, make sure to pack a fun reading book along with your school things. This way, whenever you have a few minutes free, your book is always **at hand**.

⌃ Try always carrying a book with you!

⌄ reading club

« making notes about a book

3   Second, keep a reading diary. Make notes on all the books you read: when you start and finish them, your opinions of them, some favorite lines, and so on. Seeing your list of finished books grow over time will make you excited to keep up the habit.

4   And finally, join a reading community. One of the best ways to grow your love of reading is to be around *others* who love to read. Join a reading club, either in person or online, and share your opinions about the books you have been reading. You will also get some great suggestions for future reads this way, too!

QUESTIONS

_____ 1. **Which of these has the opposite meaning to "regular" in the first paragraph?**
   (A) Rare.   (B) Usual.   (C) Difficult.   (D) Lazy.

_____ 2. **Which of these means the opposite of "at hand"?**
   (A) Close by.   (B) Next door.   (C) Far away.   (D) At once.

_____ 3. **What does "the habit" mean in the third paragraph?**
   (A) Packing your bag.   (B) Reading books.
   (C) Making friends online.   (D) Improving your memory.

_____ 4. **What is another word for "opinions" in the fourth paragraph?**
   (A) Facts.   (B) Dreams.   (C) Wishes.   (D) Thoughts.

_____ 5. **What does the writer mean by "reads" in the final sentence?**
   (A) Friends.   (B) Clubs.   (C) Books.   (D) Notes.

25

⌄ Greenland shark

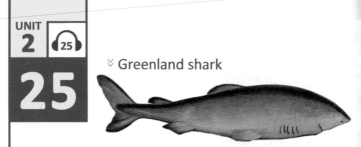

A National Favorite That's Tough to Swallow

1 It tastes a hundred times stronger than blue cheese and smells just like pee. One famous TV chef said it was "the single worst, most **disgusting** and terrible tasting thing" he had ever eaten! *Hákarl*, Icelandic rotten shark, might sound horrible to many of us, but for people in Iceland, it is a much-loved national **dish**.

2 *Hákarl* is made from the meat of the Greenland shark. When it is fresh, the meat can be deadly, so to make it **edible** it has to go through several steps. First, the shark is put in a hole in the ground and covered with sand and small stones. Then large, heavy stones are put on top to squeeze out any liquid. It stays like this for six to twelve weeks. After that, it is taken out and **hung up** to dry for several more months before it is ready to be cut up and eaten.

⌃ the Viking

3 The history of eating *hákarl* goes back more than a thousand years to the Viking age. By treating shark meat in this way, the Vikings could make sure they had food when there was nothing much else to eat. Today, Icelanders are no longer **short on** food, but eating *hákarl* is a special way for them to connect with their past.

≋ *Hákarl* is made by drying the shark's meat.

≋ *Hákarl* is a much-loved national dish in Iceland.
(cc by Audrey)

Q UESTIONS

_____ 1. Which of these pictures shows someone's face after eating something "disgusting"?

(A)

(B)

(C)

(D)

_____ 2. Which of these is another word for "dish" in the first paragraph?
(A) Plate.   (B) Food.
(C) Bowl.   (D) Drink.

_____ 3. What does "edible" most likely mean?
(A) Quick to cook.   (B) Taste good.
(C) Safe to eat.   (D) Cheap to buy.

_____ 4. What is the opposite of "hang up"?
(A) Back down.   (B) Turn down.
(C) Close down.   (D) Take down.

_____ 5. What does it mean if you are "short on" something?
(A) You don't have enough of it.
(B) You aren't happy about it.
(C) You don't know how to do it.
(D) You are tired of it.

≋ *Hákarl* is cut up for eating.
(cc by Jerick Parrone)

26 A Fright at the Lake

» angry goose

1 Last weekend was unbelievable! I had a very unusual experience while I was out camping with my family.

2 My family and I took a camping trip to Lake Snoogans. While my mom and dad set up the tent, my brother and I went to the lake to explore and see what was around. We saw a large bush and could hear strange sounds coming from it. We decided to find out what it was, so we crept closer to the bush. We tried to be very quiet. We didn't want to surprise any animal that might be hiding inside. Then, my brother coughed! A big goose shot from the bush,

⌃ climbing up a tree

⌄ bush

Q UESTIONS

_____ 1. **Which word means the same as "unusual"?**
(A) Common. (B) Strange. (C) Real. (D) Boring.

_____ 2. **Which word means the opposite of "aggressive"?**
(A) Friendly. (B) Beautiful. (C) Smart. (D) Proud.

_____ 3. **In the story, "a big goose shot from the bush." What does that phrase mean?**
(A) It jumped into the bush. (B) It threw things from the bush.
(C) It hid inside the bush. (D) It ran out of the bush.

_____ 4. **What does "around" in the second paragraph refer to?**
(A) In a circle. (B) Covering everything.
(C) In the area nearby. (D) Up and down.

camping by the lake

making a terrible sound, and it came right for me! I turned and ran as fast as I could, but the goose kept chasing me and flapping its wings crazily. I found a tree and quickly climbed up. Luckily the goose didn't follow me up the tree and decided to walk away.

3   I had better do some research on how to deal with an angry goose, so that I can be ready for next time. I had no idea they could be so aggressive!

Here are some **tips** on what to do if you meet an angry goose.

- Back away slowly. If you run, the goose will chase you.
- Don't get scared. It will make the goose excited.
- Don't turn your back on the goose. Keep watching it carefully.
- If a goose bites you, go to a doctor.

Remember the goose is probably just scared.
If you show you are not a danger, it will leave you alone.

_____ 5. **Once home, the writer read this web page (see above).
What does "tips" mean on this web page?**

(A) Sharp points. (B) Ideas to help you.

(C) Push things over. (D) Hit something.

27 Field Trip to the Farm

» feeding a goat

Hill Valley High School Notice   March 3, 2022

Field Trip to Sunnydale Farm

1 Dear Parents,

2   The eighth-grade students are going to go on a field trip to Sunnydale Farm. Everyone will gather outside the school, and the school bus will take us to the farm.

3   Once **there**, the students can feed some of the animals. After lunch, they are going to learn how to plant crops, like rice and corn. It is a great **opportunity** for the students to experience the **way of life** on a farm and understand more about what farmers do every day. The school bus will **bring** the students **back** to school before the end of the day.

4   📅 **Date: Wednesday, April 6th**
      🕐 **Time: 8:00 a.m. – 3:30 p.m.**
      📍 **Place: Sunnydale Farm**

» Remember to prepare lunch!

5   Please prepare lunch for your child, as there is nowhere to buy food at the farm. We recommend that the students wear their PE clothes and some strong, **suitable** shoes. To sign up, please fill in the form attached to this notice and return it, so that we know how many students will be joining the trip. We hope that this will be a fun and exciting trip for everyone.

      Sincerely,
      Mr. Evans

Q UESTIONS

_____ 1. **Which of these words means the same as "opportunity?"**
   (A) Chance.
   (B) Hope.
   (C) Fun.
   (D) Win.

_____ 2. **The school bus will bring the students back to school. What is the opposite of "bring back"?**
   (A) Take away.
   (B) Give back.
   (C) Give away.
   (D) Come from.

_____ 3. **What place does the word "there" in the third paragraph refer to?**
   (A) The school bus.
   (B) Hill Valley High School.
   (C) The farm.
   (D) Outside of school.

_____ 4. **Which of these means the same as "suitable"?**
   (A) Correct for use.
   (B) Comfortable to wear.
   (C) Interesting to look at.
   (D) Difficult to take off.

_____ 5. **What does "way of life" mean?**
   (A) The things animals do.
   (B) How to get to the farm.
   (C) How people live.
   (D) Animals being born.

⌄ PE (physical education) clothes

« strong shoes

crops

⌃ rice

» corn

28 Learning Skills for Life

How to Be an Adult: A Guide for Teenagers
By Kenny Chang

Preface

1 **R**ight now, you are a teenager. You have to spend hours every day at school. You worry about your grades and your friendship groups. I understand that life as a teenager can be hard. But soon, you'll become an adult. And take it from me, things don't get any easier! As an adult, you have so many responsibilities. You have to be able to feed yourself, clothe yourself, and pay the rent, to name just a few. When I went through the change from being a teenager to an adult, I found it almost overwhelming!

QUESTIONS

_____ 1. **Which of these is the opposite of "adult"?**
(A) Writer.   (B) Teacher.   (C) Child.   (D) Father.

_____ 2. **What does the writer mean by "take it from me"?**
(A) Don't take me seriously because I am only joking.
(B) Please help me because I don't know what I'm doing.
(C) Believe what I say because I have experienced it.
(D) Leave me alone. I don't want to talk about it.

_____ 3. **What does "just a few" in the first paragraph refer to?**
(A) Responsibilities.   (B) Skills.
(C) Friendship groups.   (D) Readers.

2   In this book, I want to teach you, my teenage readers, all the skills I wish I knew when I was your age. If you learn these things now, you will have a much easier time as an adult.

3   Of course, I can't answer all of life's hard questions, such as "What's the meaning of life?" But I can teach you how to save money, how to buy groceries and prepare healthy meals, how to throw a fun party, and much more!

4   After reading this book, hopefully you will feel much more confident and independent. So when you do finally become an adult, you won't feel quite as lost as I did.

_____ 4. **Which of these pictures shows "groceries"?**

(A)   (B)   (C)   (D)

_____ 5. **What is another word for "lost"?**

(A) Confused.   (B) Tired.   (C) Lonely.   (D) Careless.

29 Something to Say? Post It on the Board!

Need Help with English?
I Need Help with Math!

Maybe we can help each other.

I can **assist** you with any difficult grammar problems and work with you on your English writing skills.

You can help me understand some **tricky** areas of math.

Maybe we can meet during lunchtime or after school.

Send me an email at mathenglishswap@gmail.com

Jenny Kim, **grade 8**

FOR SALE: Science Fiction Books

My older brother is moving out and he's getting rid of many of his old science fiction books. There are plenty to choose from. Just $1.5 **per** book! A list of available books can be found at www.mybrothersbooks.freesites.com

Send me a message through the website or come talk to me during break if you're interested.

Kenny Choi, grade 9

Baking Club

Do you wish you knew how to bake?
Come and join our baking club.
We meet every Wednesday at lunchtime.
Talk to Mrs. Park in classroom 203
if you'd like to **take part**!
We make all kinds of delicious cakes and cookies
that you can share with your friends or take home!

QUESTIONS

_____ 1. **Which of these is another word for "assist"?**

(A) Help.　　(B) Understand. (C) Send.　　(D) Need.

_____ 2. **What does "take part" mean in the reading?**

(A) Talk to Mrs. Park.　　(B) Join the baking club.

(C) Take some cookies home.　(D) Share cookies with friends.

_____ 3. **Which of these is the opposite of "tricky"?**

(A) Difficult.　(B) Strange.　　(C) New.　　(D) Simple.

_____ 4. **What does the word "per" most likely mean?**

(A) For each.　(B) With each.　(C) To each.　(D) On each.

_____ 5. **This is an email that someone sent to Jenny Kim.**

New Message	_ ⤢ ✕
From	gracelee@fastmail.com
Subject	Help with English/Math

Hi Jenny,

I saw your message on the school noticeboard.

I always get the top grade in math, but my English grades are terrible. I can **get together** after school on Thursdays and Fridays for an hour. Let me know if you are interested. Thanks!

Grace Lee

What is another word for "get together"?

(A) Share.　(B) Make.　　(C) Meet.　(D) Sell.

30 Social Distancing: Saving More Than Just Human Lives

1 When you hear the phrase "social distancing," what likely comes to mind is COVID-19. But did you know that people are not the only animals on Earth who use social distancing to stay healthy?

2 Honeybees also use social distancing. At the center of a colony, you will find younger bees who take care of offspring and the queen. Older bees mostly stick to the outer part of the hive. Their job is to travel outside to forage for food from plants and bring it back to the colony. Foraging exposes them to more health risks. The distance between the two groups within the hive means that there is less contact between them. This helps to protect the colony's most prized members.

3 There is even more social distancing in colonies affected by Varroa mites. When these unwanted visitors are present, the bees will

» beehive

Varroa mite

≈ bee infected by a Varroa mite on its back (cc by Piscisgate)

≈ bees around a queen

create even more social distance. The foragers will move further toward the outside of the hive. Younger bees will move closer to the hive's center. There will also be fewer foraging dances, which can cause the mites to spread. Without these social distancing measures in place, a colony can become so weak that it cannot survive. Social distancing, whether it be bees in a colony or people in cities, saves lives!

Q UESTIONS

_____ 1. **Which of the bees is "foraging"?**

(A)　　　　　(B)　　　　　(C)　　　　　(D)

_____ 2. **What is the opposite of "prized" in the second paragraph?**

(A) Cheap. 　 (B) Ugly. 　 (C) Useless. 　 (D) Weak.

_____ 3. **What is another way to say "stick" in the second paragraph?**

(A) Stay. 　 (B) Join. 　 (C) Fly. 　 (D) Push.

_____ 4. **What does "unwanted visitors" refer to in the third paragraph?**

(A) Older bees. 　　　　　(B) Foragers.

(C) Younger bees. 　　　　(D) Varroa mites.

_____ 5. **What is another word for "measures" in the third paragraph?**

(A) Methods. 　 (B) Amounts. 　 (C) Lengths. 　 (D) Laws.

UNIT
3

Study Strategies

3-1
Visual Material

3-2
Reference Sources

Visual material like charts and graphs, and reference sources like indexes and dictionaries, all provide important information. What's more, they help you understand complicated information more quickly than you can by reading. In this unit, you will learn to use them to gather information.

31 Closed for New Year's Eve

1 New Year's Eve is a fun but busy time of year. Many people throw parties to celebrate, and some cities even put on fireworks displays. Everyone goes out to watch the fireworks light up the sky when the clock strikes twelve. As a result, there can be thousands of people on the streets, so cities have to make special plans to close roads to traffic. Usually, only some roads will be closed near the fireworks display and just for a few hours before and after midnight. This way there is not too much disruption to traffic.

2 Green City has a fireworks display each New Year's Eve. The display happens at the Green City Tower, right in the city center. Each year, the Green City government puts out a map showing people which roads will be closed during the night. Maps like this will show the name of each road and use different colored lines to show which roads will be closed.

Green City New Year's Eve Fireworks Display Traffic Rules

For safety, these areas will be closed to traffic during the following times.

Red Area
12/31 (Mon) 8 p.m. to 10 p.m.

Blue Area
12/31 (Mon) 10 p.m. to 1/1 (Tue) 3 a.m.

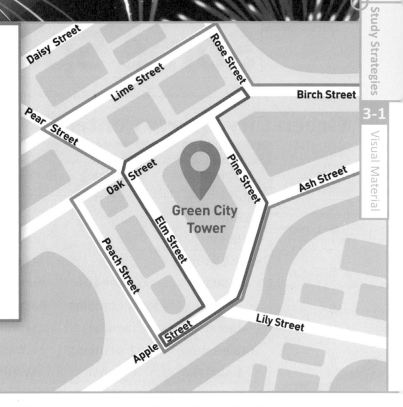

Daisy Street
Lime Street
Rose Street
Birch Street
Pear Street
Oak Street
Pine Street
Ash Street
Green City Tower
Elm Street
Peach Street
Lily Street
Apple Street

QUESTIONS

_____1. **What road will NOT be closed at all during New Year's Eve?**
(A) Daisy Street. (B) Elm Street. (C) Birch Street. (D) Oak Street.

_____2. **From what time will Peach Street be closed to traffic?**
(A) From 8 p.m. (B) From 10 p.m. (C) From 3 a.m. (D) From midnight.

_____3. **Which of the following is TRUE?**
(A) All of Oak Street will be closed for New Year's Eve.
(B) Only part of Pear Street will be closed for New Year's Eve.
(C) Elm Street will be open at 9 p.m. on New Year's Eve.
(D) Lily Street will be closed at 10 p.m. on New Year's Eve.

_____4. **On New Year's Day, starting when will traffic be allowed in the blue area?**
(A) In the afternoon. (B) Early in the morning.
(C) At midday. (D) Around dinner time.

_____5. **Jess is meeting her friends in the middle of Peach Street at 11 p.m. on New Year's Eve. Where is it OK for her to park her car?**
(A) On Elm Street. (B) On the corner of Pear Street and Oak Street.
(C) On Peach Street. (D) On Lily Street.

32 Time for Some Sport!

» playing badminton

Green City Sports Center

Time / Day	Mon.	Tue.	Wed.	Thu.	Fri.
4–5 p.m.	Badminton (under 16)	Swimming (under 16)	Rock Climbing (under 16)	Yoga (under 16)	Badminton (under 16)
5–6 p.m.	Swimming (adults)	Badminton (adults)	Swimming (under 16)	Badminton (under 16)	Rock Climbing (under 16)
6–7 p.m.	Rock Climbing (adults)	Yoga (under 16)	Table Tennis (under 16)	Swimming (adults)	Yoga (under 16)
7–8 p.m.	Yoga (adults)	Rock Climbing (adults)	Badminton (adults)	Table Tennis (under 16)	Table Tennis (adults)
8–9 p.m.	Table Tennis (adults)	Rock Climbing (adults)	Yoga (adults)	Table Tennis (adults)	Swimming (adults)

Under 16 classes: US$10/hour   **Adult classes:** US$18/hour
Limit 20 people per class.

« table tennis

1 If you live in a big city, it can be hard to find a good place to exercise. Outside, there is lots of traffic, and the air can be bad to breathe. But if you are lucky, there will be a sports center near where you live. Sports centers have many great facilities that allow people to exercise in a safe environment.

2 Sports centers also often hold classes during the day so that young people and adults can learn to do certain activities with a teacher. These might include yoga classes, swimming classes, table tennis classes, and many more. You can find details about these classes on your sports center's class schedule. A schedule (see above) shows you

« yoga class

Evening Class Days/Times
(Until **September 1**)

Sat.	Sun.
Table Tennis (under 16)	Rock Climbing (under 16)
Swimming (under 16)	Table Tennis (adults)
Rock Climbing (adults)	Yoga (adults)
Badminton (adults)	Swimming (adults)
Yoga (adults)	Badminton (adults)

* To join a class, please ask at the front desk.

when a class takes place each week. It should also include details about prices and class size limits.

3 Why not visit your local sports center and pick up one of their class schedules? See if there are any that seem interesting to you. You might find your new favorite sport!

QUESTIONS

_____ 1. **On which of the following days/ times is there a yoga class at the Green City Sports Center?**
(A) Friday, 6–7 p.m.
(B) Saturday, 4–5 p.m.
(C) Monday, 5–6 p.m.
(D) Tuesday, 7–8 p.m.

_____ 2. **What is TRUE about the swimming class on Sunday at 7 p.m.?**
(A) It is free.
(B) More than 20 people can join.
(C) It is only for adults.
(D) It is for people under the age of 16.

_____ 3. **What will probably happen after September 1?**
(A) The class prices will change.
(B) The class sizes will change.
(C) The activities will change.
(D) The class days and times will change.

_____ 4. **When on Thursday could a person under 16 take a table tennis class?**
(A) 4–5 p.m.   (B) 5–6 p.m.
(C) 7–8 p.m.   (D) 8–9 p.m.

_____ 5. **On which of these days/times could an adult NOT take a rock climbing class?**
(A) Tuesday, 8–9 p.m.
(B) Sunday, 4–5 p.m.
(C) Saturday, 6–7 p.m.
(D) Monday, 6–7 p.m.

33 A Big Boost for Food Delivery

1 Due to COVID-19, 2020 was a bad year for many businesses. But one industry that grew a great deal in that year was food delivery. With many places closed for eating inside, people turned to food delivery apps to get meals sent to their homes.

2 Even in Taiwan, where restaurants stayed open during 2020, food delivery services still grew a lot. Many people in Taiwan used these apps because they did not want to gather in large groups. Getting food sent to one's home was a good way to avoid people and lower one's risk of getting COVID-19.

3 In one survey, Internet users in Taiwan were asked about their food delivery habits during the first half of 2020. The pie chart on the next page shows how they answered. A pie chart shows amounts as pieces of a circle or "pie." The larger the amount, the larger the slice of the pie. As you can see, almost 11% had food sent home for the first time in the first half of 2020! What a boost!

» By using food delivery services, people can avoid gathering in groups.

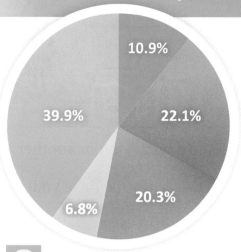

Food Delivery Habits During the First Half of 2020

(Source: MIC, Institute for Information Industry)

10.9%

39.9%

22.1%

20.3%

6.8%

- ● Never ordered food delivery before COVID-19 but started during the first half of 2020.
- ● Ordered food delivery before COVID-19 and increased the number of orders during the first half of 2020.
- ● Ordered food delivery before COVID-19 but did not increase the number of orders during the first half of 2020.
- ● Ordered food delivery before COVID-19 but never during the first half of 2020.
- ● Never ordered food delivery before COVID-19 and never during the first half of 2020.

Q UESTIONS

_____1. **What color slice shows the amount of people who ordered food delivery before COVID-19 but never during the first half of 2020?**
   (A) Orange.　　(B) Grey.　　(C) Green.　　(D) Yellow.

_____2. **What does the blue slice show?**
   (A) The amount of people who never ordered food delivery before COVID-19 but started during the first half of 2020.
   (B) The amount of people who ordered food delivery before COVID-19 and increased the number of their orders in the first half of 2020.
   (C) The amount of people who never ordered food delivery before COVID-19 and never during the first half of 2020.
   (D) The amount of people who ordered food delivery before COVID-19 but did not increase the number of their orders in the first half of 2020.

_____3. **What amount of people asked in the survey ordered food delivery before COVID-19 and increased the number of their orders in the first half of 2020?**
   (A) 20.3%　　　(B) 22.1%　　　(C) 6.8%　　　(D) 39.9%

_____4. **Which color slices show people who did order food delivery in the first half of 2020?**
   (A) Yellow, blue, and green.　　(B) Green, orange, and grey.
   (C) Grey, yellow, and orange.　　(D) Blue, green, and grey.

_____5. **What percentage of people asked in the survey ordered food delivery before COVID-19?**
   (A) Over 50%.　　　　　　(B) Less than 50%.
   (C) More than 75%.　　　　(D) Less than 25%.

The Cost of Living

1 Would you like to live abroad some day? Living in another country can be a great experience. It can really increase your understanding of the world and help you grow as a person. One important thing to think about before you decide where you want to live is the cost of living.

2 The cost of living is the amount of money you need to pay for important everyday things. These include your rent, your food, and utilities such as water, gas, and electricity. In fact, these three things make up most of the cost of living in big cities. But there are also things like clothing, public transport, and fun activities to think about, too.

3 Look at the bar graph on the next page. It shows the cities in the world with the highest cost of living. A bar graph shows numbers as bars of different lengths. The higher the number, the longer the bar. This makes it easy to compare different numbers.

≽ utilities

≽ San Francisco

Estimated Monthly Cost of Living in the World's Most Expensive Cities*

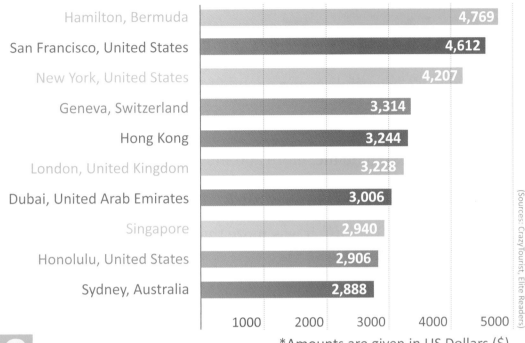

Hamilton, Bermuda — 4,769
San Francisco, United States — 4,612
New York, United States — 4,207
Geneva, Switzerland — 3,314
Hong Kong — 3,244
London, United Kingdom — 3,228
Dubai, United Arab Emirates — 3,006
Singapore — 2,940
Honolulu, United States — 2,906
Sydney, Australia — 2,888

1000   2000   3000   4000   5000

*Amounts are given in US Dollars ($).

(Sources: CrazyTourist, Elite Readers)

QUESTIONS

_____1. **How much money each month would you need to live in Geneva, Switzerland?**
(A) Around $2,888.   (B) Around $3,314.
(C) Around $4,769.   (D) Around $4,207.

_____2. **Which of the following cities is the most expensive to live in?**
(A) London.   (B) Singapore.   (C) Sydney.   (D) Hong Kong.

_____3. **In which city would you need $4,207 each month to live?**
(A) Honolulu.   (B) New York.   (C) Dubai.   (D) Hamilton.

_____4. **Which country has more cities in the top ten world's most expensive cities list than any other?**
(A) United States.   (B) United Kingdom.
(C) Australia.   (D) Switzerland.

_____5. **Which of the following is TRUE?**
(A) San Francisco has the highest cost of living in the world.
(B) The cost of living in Hong Kong is double that in London.
(C) It is cheaper to live in Singapore than in Dubai.
(D) Sydney has the lowest cost of living in the world.

🎧 35

35

Visitors From Abroad

1 Taiwan's beautiful scenery, good food, and friendly people make this place a great place for tourists. Before the COVID-19 pandemic, more and more people were visiting Taiwan each year. In 2010, 5.7 million tourists visited Taiwan. In 2019, it was more than 11 million!

2 Most visitors to Taiwan come from other Asian places, such as mainland China, Hong Kong, Japan, South Korea, and Malaysia. Flights between these places and Taiwan are short and cheap. Visitors also like how safe Taiwan is, the low cost of goods, and the relaxed atmosphere.

⌃ Taiwanese
bubble tea
(cc by Howief)

3 On the next page is a line graph that shows the number of visitors to Taiwan from these five places. A line graph shows numbers as points joined by a line. By looking at the shape of the line, you can see how the numbers go up or down over time. The numbers start in 2012 and end in 2021. In 2020, Taiwan was closed to tourists because of COVID-19. This is why the numbers have dropped so much over the last two years.

⌄ Asian tourists
in Jiufen

Changes in the Number of Visitor Arrivals from Japan, South Korea, Malaysia, Mainland China, and Hong Kong from 2012 to 2021

(Unit: Persons)

4,000,000
3,500,000
3,000,000
2,500,000
2,000,000
1,500,000
1,000,000
500,000
0

2012 2013 2014 2015 2016 2017 2018 2019 2020 2021 (Unit: Year)

Hong Kong   Mainland China   Japan   South Korea   Malaysia   Others

(Source: https://stat.taiwan.net.tw/)

QUESTIONS

_____1. How many tourists from South Korea visited Taiwan in 2017?
   (A) Just below 500,000.   (B) Around 1,250,000.
   (C) Just over 1,000,000.   (D) Just over 1,500,000.

_____2. In 2014, nearly 4 million tourists came to Taiwan from which place?
   (A) Mainland China.   (B) South Korea.   (C) Japan.   (D) Hong Kong.

_____3. Between 2012 and 2019, the number of tourists from which of these places grew the least?
   (A) South Korea.   (B) Japan.   (C) Hong Kong.   (D) Malaysia.

_____4. Which of the following is TRUE?
   (A) In 2019, more tourists from Japan visited Taiwan than tourists from mainland China.
   (B) In 2012, more tourists from South Korea visited Taiwan than tourists from Malaysia.
   (C) In 2014, more tourists visited Taiwan from mainland China than from anywhere else in the world.
   (D) In 2020, the total number of tourists that visited Taiwan was zero.

_____5. What was the change in the number of tourists from mainland China between 2015 and 2017?
   (A) The number grew by more than a million.
   (B) The number fell by more than a million.
   (C) The number stayed the same.
   (D) The number fell by half a million.

093

36 An Age of War

⌃ "peace, not war" poster

1. In 2022, Russia attacked its neighbor Ukraine. The news shocked many. We are not even halfway through the 21st century and already there have been several large wars. At the end of the last century, many hoped that the new century would be a more peaceful one. The 20th century was a very bloody hundred years with many terrible wars.

2. During World Wars I and II, countries from all around the world fought each other. This had never happened before the 20th century. There were many bloody local wars, too, where people from the same country fought each other. The Spanish Civil War and the Chinese Civil War are just two out of many examples.

3. Take a look at the timeline on the next page. A timeline lists events from earliest to latest. This timeline shows the major wars of the modern age. The years are shown at the top. The wars are shown below. You can see how long each lasted by looking at the purple bars. Let's hope the 21st century does not continue in the same way as the last one.

⌄ people hiding under a bridge in Ukraine (cc by mvs.gov.ua)

Major Wars of the 20th and 21st Centuries

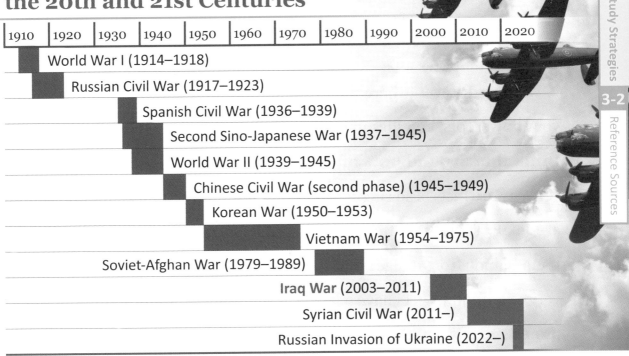

1910	1920	1930	1940	1950	1960	1970	1980	1990	2000	2010	2020

World War I (1914–1918)

Russian Civil War (1917–1923)

Spanish Civil War (1936–1939)

Second Sino-Japanese War (1937–1945)

World War II (1939–1945)

Chinese Civil War (second phase) (1945–1949)

Korean War (1950–1953)

Vietnam War (1954–1975)

Soviet-Afghan War (1979–1989)

Iraq War (2003–2011)

Syrian Civil War (2011–)

Russian Invasion of Ukraine (2022–)

QUESTIONS

_____ 1. **What does the timeline NOT show?**

    (A) The name of each war.   (B) When each war started.

    (C) When each war ended.   (D) How many people died in each war.

_____ 2. **Which of these wars lasted the longest?**

    (A) The Vietnam War.   (B) The Chinese Civil War.

    (C) The Iraq War.   (D) World War I.

_____ 3. **Which of the following wars began first?**

    (A) World War II.   (B) The Vietnam War.

    (C) The Spanish Civil War.   (D) The Korean War.

_____ 4. **Which two wars began in the 1950s?**

    (A) The Korean War and the Vietnam War.

    (B) World War I and World War II.

    (C) The Syrian Civil War and the Soviet-Afghan War.

    (D) The Spanish Civil War and the Chinese Civil War.

_____ 5. **How long did the Iraq War last?**

    (A) Eight years.   (B) Ten years.   (C) Five years.   (D) Four years.

UNIT 3

37

» Insects have a hard skeleton outside. (cc by Lsadonkey)

37 Insects Are Everywhere!

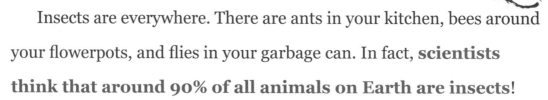

1   Insects are everywhere. There are ants in your kitchen, bees around your flowerpots, and flies in your garbage can. In fact, **scientists think that around 90% of all animals on Earth are insects**!

2   Why are insects so successful? One reason is their size. Insects are small. This means they need less energy to live, and it is easier for them to hide from danger. But despite their small size, they are also very tough. All insects have a hard skeleton outside their body that protects them from getting hurt. With all of these advantages, it is no wonder that insects rule the world!

3   There are many great books out there that you can read to learn more about insects. When shopping for a good book, take a look at the table of contents in the front. (Here is an example from the book *Inside the Insect World*). It tells you the name of each chapter and the page on which it starts. By looking at the table of contents, you can get a good idea of whether the book will interest you.

⌄ Most of the animals on Earth are insects.

Inside the Insect World

Contents

QUESTIONS

_____1. **On which page does "Chapter 8: Insect Colors" begin?**
(A) Page 96.   (B) Page 45.   (C) Page 112. (D) Page 8.

_____2. **In which chapter would you learn about how insects change as they grow?**
(A) Chapter 5.   (B) Chapter 3.   (C) Chapter 7.   (D) Chapter 10.

_____3. **In the first paragraph, the writer says, "scientists think that around 90% of all animals on Earth are insects!" In which chapter of the book Inside the Insect World would you most likely find this fact?**
(A) Chapter 9.   (B) Chapter 2.   (C) Chapter 4.   (D) Chapter 1.

_____4. **Which of these is TRUE about Chapter 9?**
(A) It is 10 pages long.   (B) It covers two main topics.
(C) It is about insect bodies.   (D) It is the final chapter of the book.

_____5. **Which page should you turn to if you are interested in how insects send messages to each other?**
(A) Page 96.   (B) Page 60.   (C) Page 18.   (D) Page 140.

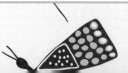

38 The Art of Folding Paper

1   The Japanese art of *origami*, or paper folding, is very easy to explain. All you need is a piece of paper and a little patience. By folding the paper again and again, you can create a beautiful object. This could be anything, but animals are most common. Some basic designs, like the popular paper crane, can be done in no time at all. Harder ones, on the other hand, need a lot of skill. These can take a very long time to finish.

2   Do you want to learn more about the history of paper folding or maybe learn how to do it yourself? If so, a good place to start is an Internet search engine. When you do the search, you'll get a list of results. Each one shows the site address on top. Below that are some details about what you can find there. Here's an example of what you might get if you type "origami" into a search engine.

QUESTIONS

_____ 1. **You want to learn about the history of *origami*. Which site do you visit?**
   (A) www.origamiforkids.com
   (B) www.everythingjapan.com.jp
   (C) www.thepaperstore.com
   (D) www.localteacher.com

_____ 2. **What would you find on the site www.how-to-origami.com?**
   (A) A choice of *origami* designs to follow online.
   (B) A list of *origami* teachers who live near you.
   (C) Different kinds of *origami* paper that you can buy.
   (D) A history of how *origami* was used in Japanese weddings.

www.how-to-origami.com
Learn Origami Today

Learn how to fold lots of cool origami models. We have clear steps and photos for each one. Check out our library of over 1,000 origami designs, from basic to hard!

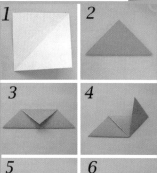

www.everythingjapan.com.jp/origami/history
The Story of Origami

Origami has a long history in Japan. The first time origami was written about was in 1680 in a poem by **Ihara Saikaku**. The poem talks about a paper butterfly design that was often used in weddings . . .

www.origamiforkids.com
30+ Easy, Cute Origami Designs

Check out our 30+ origami designs that young children will find easy to do. They're also super cute! We have rabbits, frogs, teddy bears, and more!

www.thepaperstore.com/origami-paper
Paper for Origami in All Sizes and Colors

Looking for origami paper? We have a huge selection, all at low prices. Our origami paper is thin and easy to fold . . .

www.localteacher.com/arts/origami
Find Origami Teachers Near You

Take origami classes for just $15 an hour. The first lesson is free. All levels welcome.

_____3. **You want to show your five-year-old sister some easy *origami*. Which site do you visit?**

(A) www.everythingjapan.com.jp (B) www.thepaperstore.com

(C) www.localteacher.com (D) www.origamiforkids.com

_____4. **What is TRUE about the items for sale at** www.thepaperstore.com/origami-paper**?**

(A) They are all white. (B) They only come in one size.

(C) They are not expensive. (D) They are difficult to work with.

_____5. **What do we know about Ihara Saikaku?**

(A) He was born in 1680. (B) He was a famous *origami* designer.

(C) He lived in the 20th century. (D) He wrote a poem about *origami*.

39

» Happy people can make others happy.

Don't Worry, Be Happy!

1   Are you happy? It is a simple question but an important one. Studies have shown that being happy results in people working better, having better health, and saving more money. In short, if you are happy, you will often do better in life. What's more, happy people tend to make others happy, which in turn makes more people happy, and so on. You being happy, then, is not just good for you; it is good for everyone!

2   In English, there are many ways to be happy. You could be *joyful*, *cheery*, *merry*, or *sunny*, to name but a few. To see all the ways you can describe yourself as "happy," look in a thesaurus. A thesaurus is a little bit like a dictionary. If you look up a word, you will find its meaning.

QUESTIONS

_____1. **Which of these is TRUE about the word fortunate?**
    (A) It is an antonym of *happy* (meaning *lucky and convenient*).
    (B) It is a synonym of *happy* (meaning *feeling or showing pleasure*).
    (C) It is a synonym of *happy* (meaning *lucky and convenient*).
    (D) It is an antonym of *happy* (meaning *feeling or showing pleasure*).

_____2. **Which of these words mean the opposite of *happy* (meaning *willing to do something*)?**
    (A) Delighted.   (B) Joyless.   (C) Reluctant.   (D) Inconvenient.

happy

1. ***a.*** feeling or showing pleasure
   - *Having lots of good friends made Jack very happy.*

   SYNONYMS: blissful, cheerful, cheery, delighted, glad, joyful, merry, pleased, satisfied, sunny, thankful
   ANTONYMS: displeased, joyless, sad, unhappy

2. ***a.*** willing to do something
   - *The workers at the supermarket are always happy to help customers.*

   SYNONYMS: contented, delighted, glad, pleased, ready, willing
   ANTONYMS: reluctant, unwilling

3. ***a.*** lucky and convenient
   - *The two of us meeting today in the park was a happy accident.*

   SYNONYMS: convenient, felicitous, **fortunate**, lucky, opportune, timely
   ANTONYMS: inconvenient, inopportune, unfortunate, unlucky, untimely

But you will also find a list of synonyms and antonyms for that word. A synonym is a word with a similar meaning. An antonym is a word with the opposite meaning. Each entry lists synonyms and antonyms in order from A to Z.

_____3. Which word is a synonym for both *happy* (meaning *feeling or showing pleasure*) and *happy* (meaning *willing to do something*)?
(A) Pleased.   (B) Sad.   (C) Sunny.   (D) Timely.

_____4. Another word for *happy* (meaning *lucky and convenient*) is *auspicious*. Where would *auspicious* appear in this thesaurus entry?
(A) Before *inconvenient*.   (B) Between *contented* and *delighted*.
(C) Before *convenient*.   (D) Between *convenient* and *felicitous*.

_____5. Which of these words could replace *happy* in the sentence "Having lots of good friends made Jack very happy"?
(A) Displeased. (B) Glad.   (C) Ready.   (D) Opportune.

40 A Dish for Summer

1 When the sun is out in summer, the last thing you want is a heavy, hot meal. No, you want something light, bright, and fresh!

2 One dish that I love to make during summer is a rainbow salad. It is super simple, tasty, and healthy! The idea behind it is to use as many different colored ingredients as you can. This way you get lots of different flavors plus a ton of healthy vitamins.

3 You can make a rainbow salad out of any vegetables you want. But here's a recipe for one that I like to make. It uses simple ingredients that you can find in your local market. It also has a tasty peanut butter dressing, which adds even more flavor to the dish. The recipe has a list of everything you need to make the salad, along with a step-by-step guide on how to put it all together. Just reading the recipe is making my mouth water! Enjoy!

QUESTIONS   » salad ingredients

_____ 1. **You want to make a rainbow salad for eight people. How many heads of lettuce will you need?**
   (A) One.   (B) Two.   (C) Three.   (D) Four.

_____ 2. **Which of these do you NOT need to make this recipe?**
   (A) A knife.   (B) A large bowl.
   (C) A small bowl.   (D) A bottle opener.

_____ 3. **How much salt do you need for this recipe?**
   (A) Fifty grams.   (B) Two hundred and fifty grams.
   (C) Just a pinch.   (D) Two tablespoons.

» rainbow salad with peanut butter

Summer Rainbow Salad

Serves: 4

Time to make: 40 minutes

Ingredients:

Peanut Butter Dressing	Salad
• 3 tablespoons of smooth peanut butter	• 1 head of lettuce
• 3 tablespoons of balsamic vinegar	• ¼ head of purple cabbage
• 2 tablespoons of olive oil	• 250 g cherry tomatoes
• 1 pinch of salt	• 1 medium carrot
• 1 pinch of black pepper	• 1 medium cucumber
	• 50 g black beans
	• 1 yellow bell pepper
	• ½ red onion
	• 1 handful of fresh basil
	• 2 tablespoons of mixed nuts.

Steps:

① Cut up the lettuce, basil, cabbage, carrot, cucumber, red onion, tomatoes, and bell pepper. Put these, the black beans, and the mixed nuts into a large bowl.

② In a small bowl, mix the ingredients for the dressing.

③ Put the dressing and the salad in the fridge for 30 minutes so everything gets nice and cold.

④ After half an hour, add the dressing to the salad and mix everything together.

⑤ Serve!

» bell peppers

_____4. **When do you add the dressing to the salad?**

(A) Before you put the salad in the fridge.

(B) Just before you serve the dish.

(C) Right after you put the salad ingredients in the bowl.

(D) Thirty minutes after you serve the dish.

_____5. **You want to serve this dish for lunch at 1 p.m. When should you start making it?**

(A) At 12:20 p.m.　　(B) At 12:00 p.m.

(C) At 12:40 p.m.　　(D) At 12:50 p.m.

UNIT
4

Final Review

4-1

Review: Reading Skills

4-2

Review: Word Study

4-3

Review: Visual Material

4-4

Review: Reference Sources

In this unit, you will review what you have learned. From these comprehensive questions, you can examine how well you have absorbed the ideas and material in this book.

41 Mending the Sky

1   The Hakka people in Taiwan are known for being hard-working. But on one special day, they will set aside their work and sing traditional folk songs to celebrate. This is "Sky Mending Day," a day when the Hakkas take a day off to pay tribute to the world-saving goddess **Nuwa**.

2   According to a Chinese legend, the god of water fought the god of fire. When the god of water lost, he hit his head on a pillar that held up heaven. The pillar then fell, and heaven cracked open. This resulted in terrible disasters on Earth. All seemed lost until Nuwa appeared. Nuwa acted quickly and filled the cracks in the sky with rocks of five colors. Heaven was closed again, and peace returned to Earth.

3   Sky Mending Day is said to be the day when heaven was mended. To celebrate Nuwa fixing the sky, Hakka people often go to temples together on this day. Everyone eats glutinous rice cakes, a symbol of

≫ Hakka people worship during the Sky Mending Day celebrations.
(Source: Hakka Affairs Council)

≫ the goddess Nuwa
(cc by 阿爾特斯)

» fried sticky rice balls eaten on Sky Mending Day
(Source: New Taipei City Government)

the rocks of five colors. Fried sticky rice balls are decorated with needles and stitches, like the tools Nuwa used.

4   The day traditionally falls on the 20th day of the first month of the lunar calendar. In Taiwan, this day was once celebrated as **National Hakka Day** (now changed to December 28th, the day when the Hakka Language Restoration Movement was launched in 1988). The Taiwanese government created this special holiday to honor the Hakka people.

Q UESTIONS

_____ 1. **What is the writer's purpose of the article?**
    (A) To tell a story.   (B) To talk about rice cakes.
    (C) To describe what Nuwa did.   (D) To introduce the holiday.

_____ 2. **What is probably TRUE about Nuwa?**
    (A) She breaks the pillar of heaven.   (B) She is powerful.
    (C) She collects rocks.   (D) She can repair a lot of things.

_____ 3. **What is the main idea of the article?**
    (A) Sky Mending Day is an important holiday for Hakka people.
    (B) The Hakka people like to eat glutinous rice cakes.
    (C) Nuwa saved the world from destruction.
    (D) The fire god fought a battle with the god of water.

_____ 4. **How does the writer end the last paragraph?**
    (A) With a story.   (B) With a reason.
    (C) With a joke.   (D) With a piece of advice.

_____ 5. **Which day did National Hakka Day fall on when it was first created?**
    (A) The first day of the twentieth lunar month.
    (B) Twenty days after January 1.
    (C) One day into the first lunar month.
    (D) The twentieth day of the first lunar month.

42 Feeding the World

1   There are around 800 million people suffering from hunger in the world today. One group that is doing its best to reduce that number is the World Food Programme (WFP). The WFP serves the hungry in 117 countries. One of its main operations is to provide emergency food to those in areas affected by war.

WFP

⌃ logo of the WFP

2   The WFP believes that war and hunger go hand in hand. When a war begins, many people are driven from their homes and their land. Without land to grow food or money to buy it, people are more likely to go hungry. However, hunger often also causes wars to start. If people are unhappy because they are hungry, then they are more likely to turn to violence. Solving hunger, then, is an important step in bringing peace to the world.

3   To achieve this goal, the WFP works to provide regular meals to those in poor communities around the world. If war breaks out, the WFP provides food to those caught up in the fighting. And when war ends, the WFP stays to help people rebuild their lives. Because of its efforts, the WFP was given the Nobel Peace Prize in 2020. For all its great work, it certainly deserved it!

⌄ WFP's food package
(cc by Korzhiv1)

⌄ South Sudanese people receiving help from the WFP
(cc by United Nations Photo)

« The WFP provides food for refugees in Ethiopia.

Q UESTIONS

_____ 1. **How does the writer create interest in the first paragraph?**
   (A) With a personal story.   (B) With a strong opinion.
   (C) With a play on words.   (D) With a surprising number.

_____ 2. **Which of the following sentences from the article shows the writer's bias?**
   (A) The WFP serves the hungry in 117 countries.
   (B) For all its great work, it certainly deserved it!
   (C) The WFP believes that war and hunger go hand in hand.
   (D) Because of its efforts, the WFP was given the Nobel Peace Prize.

_____ 3. **What is the writer's tone in the article?**
   (A) Serious.   (B) Bitter.   (C) Scared.   (D) Excited.

_____ 4. **What is the main idea of the second paragraph?**
   (A) When a war begins, many people are driven from their homes.
   (B) Solving hunger can help bring about peace.
   (C) If people are hungry, they are more likely to turn to violence.
   (D) The WFP often works in areas affected by war.

_____ 5. **Look at the following table. Which number should go in the blank space?**

Groups That Have Won the Nobel Peace Prize Since 2010	
Group	**Year**
European Union	2012
Organisation for the Prohibition of Chemical Weapons	2013
Tunisian National Dialogue Quartet	2015
International Campaign to Abolish Nuclear Weapons	2017
World Food Programme	?

   (A) 2018   (B) 2019   (C) 2020   (D) 2021

Deep Blue Mysteries

1   You may have heard of black holes, those strange dark objects in deep space. But what about blue holes? Blue holes are also very strange, though they can be found much closer to home.

2   Blue holes are deep, vertical holes found in the ocean. From above, they appear as a dark blue circle of water surrounded by the lighter blue of the open ocean. But they can go down for hundreds of meters. The deepest blue hole in the world, found between Vietnam and the Philippines in the South China Sea, is over 300 meters deep! It shouldn't come as a surprise that blue holes are very popular places for divers. However, diving in blue holes can be deadly. One blue hole in Egypt has been named the "Divers' Cemetery" because more than 40 divers have died there.

3   As well as being popular spots for divers, blue holes are popular with scientists, too. The environment inside blue holes is very interesting. At the bottom, there is hardly any light or oxygen. However, tiny life forms, such as bacteria, do still exist in these dark places. Studying these life forms can give scientists an idea of what life might look like on other planets, where conditions are very different from Earth.

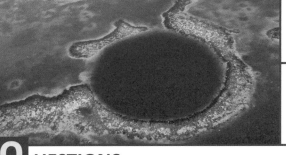

« Great Blue Hole
off the coast of Belize

» diving in a blue hole

Q UESTIONS

_____1. **How does the writer create interest in the first paragraph?**
   (A) By telling the reader a personal story.
   (B) By telling the reader a surprising number.
   (C) By making the reader curious.
   (D) By making the reader think about a problem.

_____2. **Why does the writer mention the blue hole in Egypt at the end of the second paragraph?**
   (A) To show how old blue holes can be.
   (B) To show how beautiful blue holes can be.
   (C) To show how deep blue holes can be.
   (D) To show how dangerous blue holes can be.

_____3. **Which spot on the map shows where the world's deepest blue hole is?**
   (A) **A**
   (B) **B**
   (C) **C**
   (D) **D**

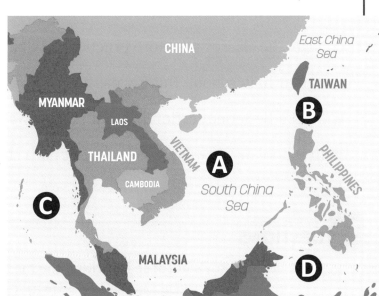

_____4. **What is the main idea of the third paragraph?**
   (A) The bottoms of blue holes are especially interesting.
   (B) There is hardly any light or oxygen inside blue holes.
   (C) Studying the environment inside blue holes is very useful to scientists.
   (D) Conditions on other planets are very different from those on Earth.

_____5. **Which of the following is likely TRUE at the bottom of blue holes?**
   (A) There are many trees down there.   (B) It is very hot down there.
   (C) There are no large fish down there.   (D) There is no water down there.

The Next Step

Dear Uncle Mike,

I have a difficult question that I need your help with. I am going to graduate from junior high school next year, but I'm not sure what to do next. Should I try to get into a regular high school and, after that, university? Or should I go to a vocational high school or five-year junior college instead? At a regular high school, the classes are more academic, and at a vocational high school or five-year junior college, the classes are more practical. My parents want me to go to a regular high school. But my passion is working with cars. I think I will get a better education in what I really want to do at a vocational high school or five-year college. What path should I take?

Roy

QUESTIONS

_____ 1. **What is Roy's purpose in writing the message?**
(A) To thank Uncle Mike.
(B) To ask Uncle Mike for advice.
(C) To offer to help Uncle Mike.
(D) To ask about Uncle Mike's job.

_____ 2. **What does Roy love to do?**
(A) Do math problems.
(B) Paint and draw.
(C) Write stories.
(D) Work with cars.

_____ 3. **What is probably TRUE about Uncle Mike?**
(A) He does not like to travel.
(B) He can fly an airplane.
(C) He likes working with people
(D) He wants to quit his job.

↑↗ academic vs. vocational education

Dear Roy,

That's a great question. I'm happy you are thinking hard about your education. As you know, I have a wonderful job as a tour guide. I take people from all over the world to see Taiwan's beautiful sights. I went to a five-year junior college, and I don't regret it. I learned a lot of great skills that helped me get my dream job. If you have a strong idea of what you want to do, then get the education that will let you follow that dream.

I hope I've been helpful!

Uncle Mike

_____ 4. **Which of the following is a biased sentence?**
   (A) I have a wonderful job as a tour guide.
   (B) I hope I've been helpful!
   (C) I am going to graduate from junior high school next year.
   (D) My parents want me to go to a regular high school.

_____ 5. **What is the main idea of Uncle Mike's reply?**
   (A) Uncle Mike is very happy doing his job as a tour guide.
   (B) Roy should get a practical education so he can follow his dream.
   (C) Uncle Mike went to a five-year junior college.
   (D) Roy is very smart to be thinking hard about his education.

45 Music and Studying: Do They Go Together?

1   A lot of students like to listen to music while they are studying, but does it help? Will it make it harder to remember the things you need to learn? Is it possible to listen to music and read at the same time?

2   Music can make you feel relaxed and put you in a good mood. It can help you forget the pressure of homework or **lighten up** at test time. It can also help you keep going during long study **period**s, as it adds something pleasant to the activity of studying.

⌄ Fast or loud music can create distractions.

« The right music can help you stay focused.

3   Music without words doesn't seem to affect students' memories too much. On the other hand, music that has words can create distractions and make it more difficult to focus on your task. Also, music that is too loud or too fast can influence your memory when you are preparing for a test.

4   If you want to listen to music while you are studying, choose your music wisely. You don't want to choose something that will make it harder. You could try some calm, quiet classical music to help you relax and focus at the same time.

Q UESTIONS

_____ 1. **Which of these words means the same as "period"?**
(A) Time.   (B) Lesson.   (C) Book.   (D) Test.

_____ 2. **Which of these is the opposite of "classical"?**
(A) Modern.   (B) Nice.   (C) Cool.   (D) Interesting.

_____ 3. **What does "lighten up" in the second paragraph mean?**
(A) Prepare for something.   (B) Make something brighter.
(C) Feel calmer.   (D) Make notes.

_____ 4. **Which of these words has the same meaning as "focus"?**
(A) Write.   (B) Listen.   (C) Play.   (D) Pay attention.

_____ 5. **What does "it" mean in the last paragraph?**
(A) Music.   (B) Memory.   (C) Studying.   (D) Relaxing.

46 Is Online Dating Really That Dangerous?

Ava: Do you remember that dating app I told you about? I've created a profile on it!

June: Seriously, Ava? After our last conversation I really thought you had decided not to try it!

Ava: Don't worry, June. I haven't started dating—yet.

June: Well, if you are going to do **it**, you must promise me a few things.

Ava: Sure, Mom.

June: You're lucky I'm *not* your mother!

Ava: I know exactly what you are going to say. Don't use my **real** name, and don't give anyone my address. Oh, and don't share any photos that I wouldn't want my parents to see.

June: Yes, but there's so much more. People aren't always who they say they are.

Ava: You need to **relax**, June.

June: Relax? What if you end up on a date with someone dangerous? Do you want to be killed while looking for love? Or have all your money stolen? These things happen all the time, Ava. How can I possibly relax?

« People aren't always who they say they are.

Ava: Okay, okay! I'm listening.

June: I read an article this morning. It said nearly one in five young women were found to have been threatened with physical harm when using online dating.

Ava: That's frightening. Maybe I should give this more thought before I try it out.

June: Phew!

QUESTIONS

_____ 1. **Which of these is another way to say "relax"?**
   (A) Slow down.   (B) Turn down.   (C) Cut down.   (D) Calm down.

_____ 2. **What does "it" refer to in June's second line?**
   (A) Creating a dating profile   (B) Dating online.
   (C) Making promises   (D) Having a conversation.

_____ 3. **What is the opposite of "real"?**
   (A) Special   (B) Other   (C) Fake   (D) True.

_____ 4. **What is another word for "frightening"?**
   (A) Scary   (B) Interesting   (C) Amazing   (D) Lonely.

_____ 5. **Here is Ava's onlinc dating profile (see below).**

Cutieava (17)

Do you believe in love at first sight? I sure hope not because I don't! It takes a long time to get to know someone.

A perfect first date for me would be enjoying a cup of tea together with you and my best friend. If you think that's weird, then don't bother messaging me. A girl can never be too careful these days!

What does "bother" mean?
(A) Make an effort.   (B) Cause problems.
(C) Become lazy.   (D) Do strange things.

47 » heavy smoke

Fire, Fire! Smoke, Smoke!

1   Fire can be deadly—but smoke is deadlier still. In fact, it is thought that breathing in smoke causes 50% to 80% of deaths related to fires.

2   If you were trapped in a smoke-filled room, would you know what to do? The typical advice from the fire service is to bring your body down low, but not too low. Heavy toxic gases can settle close to the floor, so you should move toward the door on your hands and knees. Follow the base of the wall with your eyes so you can find the door as quickly as possible.

3   It's sometimes said that you should cover your mouth with wet towels when escaping. However, fabrics can't keep out deadly gases, so you must not waste your time finding wet coverings. Just keep your breaths as shallow as you can.

QUESTIONS

_____ 1. **What is the opposite of "shallow"?**
     (A) Fast.   (B) Low.   (C) Thin.   (D) Deep.

_____ 2. **What does "it" mean in the fourth paragraph?**
     (A) The door.   (B) The smoke. (C) Your arm.   (D) Your mouth.

_____ 3. **What does "immediately" mean?**
     (A) Right away.   (B) Fully.   (C) By hand.   (D) Suddenly.

_____ 4. **Which word or phrase can replace "inhaling"?**
     (A) Putting on.   (B) Removing. (C) Coughing. (D) Breathing in.

« Smoke can be deadlier than fire.

⌄ Move to the window to escape from smoke.

4 When you reach the door, don't open it **immediately**. First check that there is no smoke coming from under the door and touch it briefly with your hand to see how hot **it** feels. If the fire is directly behind the door, it's not a safe exit, and you should crawl to the window instead.

5 **Inhaling** even small amounts of smoke can cause you to get sick or fall unconscious. So remember, don't take your time in a smoke-filled room.

⌃ Check if there is smoke coming from under the door.

_____5. **Which picture shows someone following advice from the second paragraph?**

(A)   (B)

(C)   (D)

48 A Whole Lot of Shaking Going On

1   You are sleeping comfortably, when suddenly you wake up to find your room shaking **back and forth** like something out of a movie. It takes you a moment to realize what is going on, and then you just feel worse: You are in the middle of a big earthquake.

2   For anyone living in Taiwan, earthquakes are **a fact of life**. The island experiences about 1,000 **felt** earthquakes per year, nearly three a day. Why is this? Well, Taiwan itself was created by the same undersea land plate movements that cause earthquakes. To the east, the Philippine Sea Plate is being pulled beneath the Eurasian Plate. To the south, on the other hand, the Eurasian Plate is being pulled under the Philippine Sea Plate. Between these two events is an active crash **zone** directly beneath Taiwan. This results in nearly constant earthquakes.

⌄ major plates around Taiwan

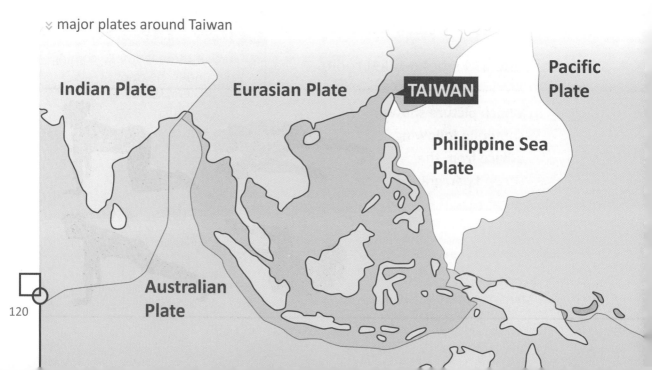

Indian Plate

Eurasian Plate

TAIWAN

Pacific Plate

Philippine Sea Plate

Australian Plate

↑ running track damaged by the 921 Earthquake (cc by Oregon State University)

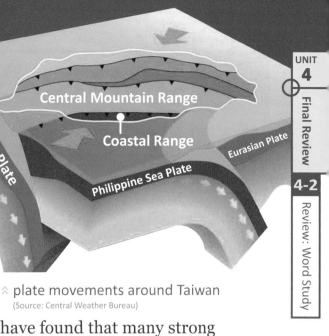

↑ plate movements around Taiwan
(Source: Central Weather Bureau)

3   Research also suggests that there may be a relationship between earthquakes and the amount of water in the ground. Scientists have found that many strong earthquakes occur during Taiwan's dry season, from February to April. Earthquake activity is at its lowest, however, between July and September at the end of the rainy season. So our little island may be unlucky **on two fronts** when it comes to shaking and quaking!

Q UESTIONS

_____ 1. **Which of the following words means the opposite of "felt" in the second paragraph?**
  (A) Feeling.   (B) Unnoticed.   (C) Quiet.   (D) Dangerous.

_____ 2. **Which of the following words has the same meaning as "zone" in the second paragraph?**
  (A) Plate.   (B) Earthquake.   (C) Island.   (D) Area.

_____ 3. **What does the phrase "back and forth" mean in the first paragraph?**
  (A) Up and down.   (B) In and out.
  (C) From side to side.   (D) From top to bottom.

_____ 4. **What does the phrase "a fact of life" mean in the second paragraph?**
  (A) Something dangerous.   (B) Something common.
  (C) Something fun.   (D) Something difficult.

_____ 5. **What does the phrase "on two fronts" mean in the third paragraph?**
  (A) In two ways.   (B) With two people.
  (C) For two countries.   (D) At two times.

49 Same Name, Different Games

1 When Americans talk about loving "football," they are usually talking about the sport where players wear helmets and throw or kick an oval ball. In this sport, the aim is for players to get the ball into the scoring area at the far end of the field. However, to people from the rest of the world, "football" means something very different. It means the game where players must kick a round ball into a goal in order to score. To avoid confusion, the former is often called "American football" and the latter "soccer."

2 For a list of what's similar and different between these two popular sports, see the Venn diagram on the next page. A Venn diagram has two circles. In the one on the next page, the left circle has facts about American football. The right one has facts about soccer. In the center, where the two circles meet, there are facts about both American football and soccer.

≫ two games sharing the same name

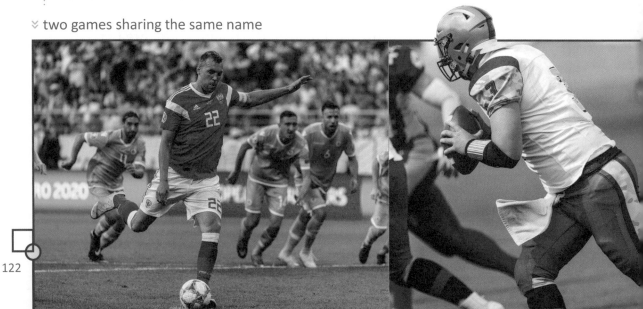

American Football

- Oval ball
- Scoring a "touchdown" gets your team 6 points.
- Players wear helmets, shoulder pads, and other protective gear.
- Players can throw or kick the ball.
- Popular mostly in North America.

- Two teams per game.
- Eleven players on each team.
- Games have a "half-time" break.
- Lots of running around.

Soccer

- Round ball
- Scoring a "goal" gets your team 1 point.
- Players wear little or no protective gear.
- Players must kick the ball (no hands, except for the goalkeepers).
- Popular around the world.

Q UESTIONS

_____1. **Which of these is TRUE about soccer?**
- (A) It is popular mostly in North America.
- (B) It uses an oval ball.
- (C) Players wear little to no protective gear.
- (D) There are ten players on a team.

_____2. **Which of these is TRUE about both soccer and American football?**
- (A) There are eleven players on each team.
- (B) Players can throw or kick the ball.
- (C) They are popular around the world.
- (D) They use a round ball.

_____3. **Which of these is NOT true about soccer?**
- (A) Players run around a lot during games.
- (B) Two teams play in each game.
- (C) Each time you score your team gets six points.
- (D) Most players must not use their hands.

_____4. **Which of these is TRUE about American football?**
- (A) Each time you score, your team gets one point.
- (B) Games have a break in the middle.
- (C) It is popular around the world.
- (D) Players can only kick the ball.

_____5. **From the Venn diagram, what can we guess about American football and soccer?**
- (A) American football players are usually shorter than soccer players.
- (B) Soccer games last longer than American football games.
- (C) Soccer players are faster runners than American football players.
- (D) American football is more dangerous than soccer.

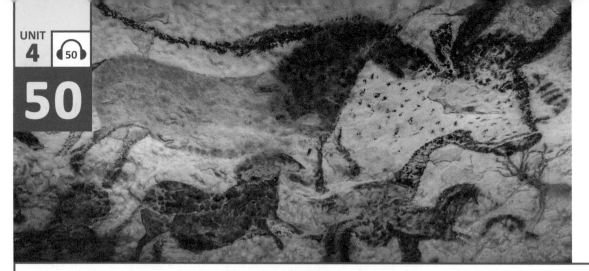

UNIT 4

50

50

Art Through Time

≫ cave painting

1   Humans have been making art for tens of thousands of years. First, we painted pictures of animals on the walls of caves. Much later, the ancient Greeks made beautiful statues of their many gods in metal and stone. In ancient China, detailed scenes with people, mountains, and rivers were painted on long scrolls. In France in the 19th century, artists tried to paint the different colors and effects of light itself. Of course, these are just a few examples.

2   To get a more complete picture of human art, why not read a book on art history? A good art history book will cover art from the ancient world to the modern. It will give you a good idea of how art has changed over time.

3   If you want to find a specific topic, take a look at the index in the back of the book. An index lists the book's topics in order from A to Z, along with the page or pages on which you can read about it. On the next page is a small part of the index from the book *Art Through Time*.

≪ ancient statue

Art Through Time, Index (Part 5)

QUESTIONS

_____ 1. On which page(s) of the book *Art Through Time* would you find information about the famous Italian painter Titian?
(A) Page 25.
(B) Pages 290 and 355.
(C) Pages 71–5.
(D) Pages 230–2.

_____ 2. What topic would you find information about on page 623?
(A) Science and art.   (B) Self-portraits.
(C) Pop Art.   (D) Roman art.

_____ 3. How many pages of the book are there on the artist Pablo Picasso?
(A) Two.   (B) Six.
(C) Seven.   (D) One.

_____ 4. What should you do if you want to find information on "Prehistoric art"?
(A) Turn to the section of index topics that begin with the letter A.
(B) Turn to the section of index topics that begin with the letter S.
(C) Turn to the section of index topics that begin with the letter C.
(D) Turn to page 314.

_____ 5. Where would the topic "Turkish art" be placed in the index section provided in the reading?
(A) Between *Tahiti* and *Terracotta army*.
(B) Between *Titian* and *Totem poles*.
(C) Between *Totem poles* and *Turner, J.M.W.*
(D) Before *Tahiti*.

Translation

※ 本書中譯採意譯，非逐字逐句翻譯，請避免逐字對照。

Unit 1 閱讀技巧

1-1 歸納要旨／找出支持性細節

01 海上飯店 P. 20

搭乘伊莉莎白郵輪，徜徉世界七大洋

您夢想過來趟極致奢華的環遊世界之旅嗎？那麼何不跟我們一同來趟輕鬆愜意的郵輪航程呢？本公司旗下的現代郵輪，就宛如漂浮在海上的五星級飯店。

白天時，郵輪上有兩座大型游泳池，任您下水徜徉。您也可以到船上的健身房鍛鍊身體，或在艙內電影院欣賞電影。夜幕低垂時，則有許多歌手、樂團及其他的表演者，包您看得不亦樂乎。

除此之外，我們的頂級廚師每天都會為您準備美味的三餐佳餚，而且每抵達一處定點，本公司將有經驗豐富的導遊，帶您遊覽所有最棒的景點，走訪道地的體驗活動、美食與文化。現在就手刀下訂，預約我們的郵輪之旅，準備好迎接您此生最美好的體驗吧！

以下為三款精彩的郵輪套裝行程，供您選擇。

歐洲航程	亞洲航程	加勒比海航程
行程時長：3週	行程時長：10天	行程時長：2週
每位價格：港幣50,000元起	每位價格：港幣25,000元起	每位價格：港幣40,000元起
旅遊國家：義大利、法國、比利時、葡萄牙、西班牙、希臘	旅遊國家：日本、南韓、新加坡、泰國、菲律賓	旅遊地點：牙買加、巴哈馬、開曼群島、百慕達、聖露西亞、貝里斯

全年皆有郵輪航班，自香港出發。
請至官網 www.elizabethcruises.com 查詢行程以及訂位資訊。

02 致我摯愛姊姊的信 P. 22

親愛的珍妮佛：

　　我有件重要的事想告訴妳，但在這之前，我希望妳知道：有妳這樣的姊姊，我真是感到無比幸運。在這個世上，妳是我最喜歡的姊姊了！還記得我們跟爸媽一起去草莓園的事嗎？妳教會我怎麼採草莓：用手指捏住莖部，然後把果實採下來。那可比逛街購物好玩多了！今年妳生日的時候，我們再去一次那裡吧！

　　妳還記得我的手指有多不靈光嗎？我把草莓捏得太用力，結果草莓就噴汁了！草莓汁濺到了妳最喜歡的外套上。我當時很怕妳會生我的氣，可是當我說對不起，妳就原諒我了。妳知道我不是故意的。

珍妮佛，妳是我心目中的超級英雄。妳不僅對我很好，對小動物也很好。我知道妳已經有好幾個月，都在動物收容所幫忙了，也許哪天，妳可以帶隻小貓咪回家！

我親愛、最愛的姊姊，我真的想跟妳說的事情是：上週妳去動物收容所幫忙的時候，我借了妳最喜歡的T恤去穿，一不小心，我就把一團番茄醬沾到衣服上了。我試過要把汙漬洗掉，可是就是洗不掉。唉呀，對不起啦！

愛妳的蔻伊

03 安德烈斯的小狗　P. 24

3月13日 星期二

今天放學回到家，爸爸給我看了一篇新聞報導。我看了之後真的很感動，所以想馬上把這件事寫下來。

那篇文章寫道，墨西哥有一家流浪狗收容所，最近在門外發現了一隻幼犬。幼犬的身邊放了一個絨毛玩具以及一張紙條，紙條是一個名叫安德烈斯的小男孩寫的。安德烈斯寫說，他會把狗狗留在收容所，是因為他爸爸會對狗狗動手動腳。他希望狗狗在收容所裡會很安全。

那間流浪狗收容所在網路上分享了此事後，有300人打電話過去，表示願意認養這隻小狗，這真是太好了。不過，收容所也提醒大家，他們還有其他120多隻狗狗同樣需要一個充滿愛的家。

這篇新聞報導真的讓我感觸良多。我有好一陣子都在問爸爸我們能不能養條狗。我以前一直想去寵物店買隻小狗，但是看了這篇報導後，我改變心意了。如果我們真的要養狗，應該要去收容所認養一隻回家。收容所有很多遭到之前的飼主傷害或遺棄的狗狗，牠們都需要溫暖的家，也許我們家就能給牠們一個好歸宿。

04 一路攀向巔峰　P. 26

凱特：嘿，傑克，我跟家人這個週末要去攀岩，你要不要跟我們一起去？

傑克：攀岩？呃，不太確定吔。

凱特：來嘛！會很好玩的！

傑克：我以前從來沒攀岩過，我擔心我會攀得一塌糊塗。

凱特：放心！那裡各種難易程度都有，你可以從初學者的牆開始，然後循序漸進。

傑克：或許可以喔，我想這個週末應該來做一些運動。

凱特：一點都沒錯！攀岩是很棒的活動，能讓你的肌肉更強而有力，而且不像有些運動那樣，會對你的關節造成負擔。

傑克：聽起來不錯嘛，我很討厭上完體育課後肌肉痠痛的感覺。

凱特：而且攀岩很有助於幫你培養身體協調性，對你這種笨手笨腳的人來說，攀岩真的很適合！

傑克：哈哈，真愛說笑😊噢，但是我星期一有數學大考，也許應該讀書才對。

凱特：攀岩對你的大腦運作也很有幫助，能夠幫助你訓練解決問題的能力。所以跟我一起去攀岩，可說就是在為你的數學考試做準備⋯⋯

傑克：好吧，既然妳都這麼說了⋯⋯ 好！我去！

凱特：好極了！晚點我會傳訊息跟你說細節。

親愛的蒂娜：

我剛看完妳的信。聽妳說妳在夏令營過得不開心，我感到相當心疼。妳想要人見人愛、受人歡迎，可是別人似乎不怎麼買帳，這肯定令人難受。我們很容易就會想說，只要改變自己的行為，轉而去迎合別人，一切問題就會迎刃而解。

妳知道嗎？我在妳這個年紀時也面臨到相同處境。我國二的時候，真的很想去上鋼琴課，但是跟我玩在一起的那群朋友，都認為學樂器一點都不酷，於是我跟他們一起加入了足球隊，因為我想讓他們喜歡我。那一年讓我過得痛不欲生，至今還是很後悔沒有去學鋼琴。

我可以用媽媽對女兒的角度，給妳一些建議嗎？別只為了得到他人的喜愛而活。有些人就是不會喜歡妳這個人。（就好比我煮的咖哩雞是人間美味，但妳就是不喜歡！）妳已經很幽默風趣、聰明伶俐而且心地善良，如果別人不了解妳，為什麼要浪費時間去討好他們呢？

記住：做你自己，才是真正的幸福所在。

最愛妳的媽媽

1-2 做出推測／釐清寫作技巧

晚安，歡迎收看九點新聞。

今晚新聞首先帶您關心：東京有兩家百貨公司本日暫停營業，原因是上週末有一名COVID-19的感染者曾去過這兩家百貨公司。

該名個案姓鈴木，是30多歲的男子，由於他即將出國出差，於是到當地醫院做了COVID-19檢測。儘管該名男子沒有出現任何症狀，但檢測結果卻呈現陽性。

該名男子接受採檢之前，曾去過住家附近的兩家百貨公司。政府已經通知同時間在場的所有人。民眾若有收到政府簡訊，皆應特別留意自身健康狀況，如果感到身體不適，請以電話聯繫當地衛生單位。

這兩家百貨公司將暫停營業24小時，同時對整棟大樓進行清潔消毒，並對全體員工實施病毒檢測。

病毒的感染源仍舊不明。該個案上個月從菲律賓出差回國，但在14天的隔離結束後，採檢結果呈現陰性。政府正全力找出他感染病毒的可能來源。

這名個案讓東京感染COVID-19的病例總數來到了16,563例。

接下來為您播報重點新聞⋯⋯

07 吉屋出租 P. 32

倫敦公寓套房，採光明亮，現正招租中，每週只要350英鎊！

這間套房一人居住綽綽有餘，內含獨立衛浴，不需和他人共用！書桌、椅子、大床、衣櫥、洗衣機、電冰箱等一應俱全。套房裡還有採光良好的大窗，另有小陽台，附有桌椅。

地點佳，近倫敦大學學院，位於熱鬧地段，商店與咖啡館林立周邊。公寓離地鐵站只需步行5分鐘，附近也有數座共享單車站。飲食方面，附近有家超市，還有許多餐廳以及多家便利超商。

禁養貓、狗等寵物，但是魚、烏龜和其他安靜的小動物則開放飼養。最短租期為一年，必須預付首月租金，並須加付押金（每月租金X2）。租金不含水電費。

如果您想要看房，請打電話給我（房東詹姆士）。我有空的時間為：週一至週五晚上6點至9點、週六或週日上午9點至晚上9點。期待您的來電！

08 幸福人生的終點站 P. 34

僅以此紀念

瓊·史密斯

1935年1月23日—2022年3月12日

在度過悠長、幸福的一生後，瓊·史密斯安詳地逝於2022年3月12日，享壽八十七歲，身後留下二子（約瑟夫與馬克）、一女（莎莉）以及七名（外）孫子女。

瓊於1935年出生在格林鎮，自小就熱愛大自然，時常攀爬樹木、採集花草，在戶外環境度過許多時光。長大後，她進入格林鎮公園管理處工作，終其一生工作不懈，致力確保格林鎮保有許多自然空間，可供大家徜徉遊憩。瓊也正是在公園管理處與羅柏相識相遇，後來羅柏就成了瓊摯愛的丈夫。

瓊深愛著她的家人，一年中她最喜歡的日子就是佳節假日，因為她的兒女跟孫子、孫女都會回家跟她一起過節。為全家人煮菜做飯令她樂此不疲，凡是品嚐過她精湛料理的人，都會深深地懷念她做的美食佳餚。最讓她開心的，就是跟孫子孫女們陪伴相處，教他們做飯並表達對他們的關愛。

瓊的喪禮茲訂於2022年3月24日（週四）下午1點，地點於亞當街教會。歡迎所有喜愛瓊的親朋好友撥空蒞臨，與瓊的家屬一起緬懷她的一生。

一步一腳印，這就是我的路線。
一步接著一步。
我會一次次告訴自己：
山之高，令我愈發堅強。

我的頭，天旋地轉；我的腳，重如石塊，
然我一步一步征服。
攻頂之際，我將心感身輕如燕！
山之高，令我愈發堅強。

遠在前方，我哥哥喊道：
「是否真遙不可及？」
四千五百三十三公尺高！
山之高，令我愈發堅強。

片刻，我俯瞰足下風光。
其下為一片雲海？我思索。
我真的已經走了這麼遠嗎？
山之高，令我愈發堅強。

見我步履維艱，父親問道：
「是否仍能砥礪前行？」
我答：「別擔心，我會繼續向前。」
山之高，令我愈發堅強。

某人道：「抱歉，你們必須折返。
峰頂因天候不佳關閉。」
吾兄泣如末日，
我卻不為所動。
山之高，已令我愈發堅強。

達文西的《蒙娜麗莎》、畢卡索的《哭泣的女人》、孟克的《吶喊》：這三幅偉大的藝術作品各自是用獨特的風格繪製而成。不過，這些畫作確實有個共同點，就是皆屬於「肖像畫」。

肖像畫是藝術史中非常重要的一環。想想照片還沒發明前的生活吧，能捕捉人像的方法不多，其中之一就是透過繪畫。古代的統治者會命令藝術家為其畫肖像畫，藉此激起臣民的敬畏之心，並讓自己在後人的記憶裡長存。後來，中產階級也開始風行花錢僱人為自己和所愛的人畫肖像畫。事實上，過去很長的一段時期裡，畫肖像畫是藝術家最佳的賺錢管道之一。

仔細觀察一幅肖像畫，可以是很奇妙的體驗。畫中人身上穿的衣服、手上拿著的物品，都向我們透露著人物的性格和其時代背景。此外，許多著名畫家，像是孟克、文森・梵谷、芙烈達・卡蘿等人，更透過將自己繪於紙上，向世界敞開他們的心靈世界。的確，肖像畫是心理學與歷史的交會點，這就是為什麼對我、對其他許多藝術愛好者來說，肖像畫是至高的藝術形式。

1-3　作者的目的及語氣／明辨寫作偏見

各位同學，三年就這樣過去了，你們相信嗎？不久之前，我們還只是傻傻的小毛頭，可是現在我們準備要上高中了！

不騙你，我剛踏進這裡的時候，心裡滿是惶恐不安。學長姊讓我望而生畏，傑克森校長更把我嚇得屁滾尿流！不過，沒多久我就發現大家其實都很親切，於是我很快就像如魚得水般，感到很自在。

本校驚才絕豔的老師們都努力傾囊相授，要給我們完善的教育，他們真的是英雄。高中生活不會輕鬆，但是本校師長已幫我們做好萬全準備。他們教會我們的不僅是學科知識，還有如何認真努力、抱持永不放棄的心。我感覺在這裡學到了很多，多到我的頭可能會爆炸，就像王老師那個瘋狂的科學實驗一樣！

我們大多都會就讀不同的高中，此後再也不會天天在一起了，這讓我感傷不已。但是我們該感到欣慰的是，自己在這所學校裡交到了這麼多好朋友。無論畢業後大家落腳何方，要知道：國中時期的朋友永遠都會在，當你的靠山。

謝謝各位，祝福大家一帆風順、鵬程萬里！

12 大自然的小幫手 P. 42 .... (cc by division, CSIRO) ▶

大自然的小幫手

本刊每月都會帶讀者認識一種對其他動、植物助益良多的神奇生物。話不多說，本期內容馬上要向各位介紹個頭雖然只有一丁點大、卻舉足輕重的糞金龜！

糞金龜（譯注：又名蜣螂、屎殼郎）是一種昆蟲，會搜集動物糞便，以此為食並築巢而居。當糞金龜發現一團美味新鮮的糞便時，就會在地上挖個洞，再把糞便完好地帶到地底下。之後，母糞金龜便會在糞便上產卵，等卵孵化後，幼蟲就以這團美味的糞便為食，直到長大成蟲。

有些人可能會覺得糞金龜很噁心，但他們這就叫做孤陋寡聞。事實上，糞金龜的行為對於動、植物大有幫助。糞金龜會把糞便帶到地底下，讓糞便與泥土混合一起，帶給土壤豐富的營養素，造福植物。此外，把糞便掩埋起來，也可避免蒼蠅在糞便產卵，這表示會傳播疾病、侵擾乳牛等可憐動物的害蟲數量，也將隨之減少。

下一期內容預告：我們將揭開在旱季時，大象如何幫助其他動物找到飲水。

13 瑞典週六糖果日 P. 44 ....

布朗教授的牙齒保健部落格

2023年11月7日 / 文：布朗教授

現今有很多小朋友滿口蛀牙，身為牙醫師的我，簡直看得怒火中燒！為什麼那些父母會這麼失職，讓自家小孩每天吃一人堆的糖果呢？

上個月，我受邀到瑞典演講時，有件事讓我很驚訝：我看到的每個小孩牙齒都很健康，然而，當地糖果店一到週六就人山人海。為何這些孩子吃這麼多甜食，卻還能維持牙齒健康呢？我請一位瑞典同仁解釋，而他說這是因為瑞典有個名為「lördagsgodis」的傳統，也就是「週六糖果日」。

根據同仁的說法，此項傳統始於1950年代。當時瑞典逐漸富裕起來，政府擔心小孩會因而吃下大量的糖分，所以建議父母將糖果當作一週一次的小確幸。很多父母從善如流，結果成效良好。如今，這已成為瑞典的一項有趣文化。小孩一整個禮拜都在期待週六去買糖果，自然也就不會因一整週天天吃糖果而毀了牙齒健康。

從這些聰明的瑞典人身上，我們可真上了一課。我衷心希望，有朝一日這個點子也能在世界各地盛行起來。

14 重修舊好 P. 46

艾蜜莉：大家好，歡迎收看本節目。朋友之間有時會起爭執，這在友誼關係當中是很正常的事情，可是發生衝突時，該如何化解芥蒂呢？我們今天很幸運邀請到了馬里博士，要給我們一些建議。

馬里博士：要處理衝突，雙方真的需要冷靜下來，人若在氣頭上，是不可能解開衝突的。其次，我們必須與對方面對面溝通。假如雙方透過別人傳話，那麼你或朋友彼此很容易會錯意，反而讓事情火上加油。

傾聽對方說話也很重要。每件事都是公說公有理，婆說婆有理！還有，我們講話時要使用「我」開頭的敘述句，讓對方知道自己的感受，例如：「我很生氣，我打電話給你都不接」，這句話可向對方確切傳達你的感受。

如果是你的錯，別忘了要道歉。許多人會拉不下臉說對不起，但是道歉代表我們知道自己做錯了。最後，我們需要和對方一起找到兩全其美的辦法來解決衝突，這是最重要的部分！

艾蜜莉：這些都是很有幫助的觀念，謝謝您！

15 女教練，在哪裡？ P. 48

在你的想像中，一名百戰百勝的球隊教練，會是男性或是女性？多數人的心目中，大概都會浮現出男性，但為什麼呢？我們知道，男性不見得更懂得為人師表，而在政壇與商界中，傑出的女性領袖紛紛輩出，那麼，為何帶領球隊的女性會這麼少呢？以美國為例，大學女子體育隊裡有60%是由男性擔任教練，但是男子體育隊裡卻只有3%是由女性執教！這種荒唐的亂象必須改變。

會認為女教練執教能力不及男教練的人，確實都應該再好好地想清楚。有聽說過派特·桑密特嗎？她在奧運籃球比賽贏得了銀牌（譯注：1976年蒙特婁奧運的女子籃球項目），後來成為美國大學籃球史上最優秀的教練之一。她帶領球隊贏得超過一千場的球賽，超越了當時大學籃球史上其他教練的紀錄。只因為是女性之故，就將出色的教練排除在外，實在不是明智之舉。試想：如果僱用技術超群、經驗豐富的女教練，而不是資質一般的男教練，球隊能多贏多少場比賽？

簡而言之，球隊管理者在選用新教練時，必須好好檢討自己的偏見。冷落女性人才，實際上是讓球隊作繭自縛之舉。

1-4 綜合技巧練習

16 「魚論」交鋒！ P. 50

在麥克老師的課堂上，學生正在進行討論。

美琪：我覺得水族館很棒啊，你可以一次近距離看到許多各式各樣、五顏六色的魚。我很喜歡跟我爸媽一起去市立水族館，每次去都玩得很開心。水族館也讓科學家研究魚類能更不費力。

彼得：我不同意。魚在海裡可以自由自在地游來游去。我認為把魚關在狹小空間裡，是很殘忍的事。我也認為對魚類來說，受到人潮的圍繞會有很大的壓力，魚也是有感覺的。

盧克：這有可能，但是海洋裡危機四伏，而在水族館裡，至少可保魚兒安全無虞。我同意美琪的看法。我們儘管住在大城市裡，卻得以如此接近大自然，我認為是好事一件。水族館讓城市人能身歷其境認識海洋生物。

蘿拉：我比較擔心水族館裡的魚有沒有受到妥善照顧。要是水族館的工作人員怠忽職守，該如何是好？我認為最好讓魚留在海洋中，那是牠們最自然的居所。

麥克老師：我認為大家在支持、反對兩方面，都提供了很棒的觀點。我們全班來投票表決吧，認為水族館是個好主意的人請舉手。

---

17 餐廳的新規定　P. 52

餐廳店長茉利亞正在舉行緊急員工會議。

○　大家早，感謝大家今天提早上班來開會。我們今天要討論一些重要事項，大家眼前都應該已經有一份重點清單。

○　首先要知會大家，我們新的營業時間會縮短。由於最近COVID-19確診數攀升，政府
○　已經要求所有餐廳要限制營業時間。我們往常的營業時間是從週二至週日、早上11點半至晚上9點，但是從下週起，我們只有下午5點到晚上9點的晚餐時段會營業，而且週
○　末會完全停止服務。這些新規定將持續至少六週。

○　我知道這表示在場許多人的工時、薪資會減少，不過請別太擔心，政府說會補助各位這段期間所有的薪資損失。我會發給你們所需文件，並在稍後的會議上教你們如何申
○　請補助。

○　好了，接下來我們要討論桌椅的重新配置，來符合保持社交距離的規定……

---

18 急尋愛犬！　P. 54

尋狗啟示！

請幫忙尋找查理！

我們家的狗狗查理在8月20日走失後，我們就再也沒見到牠的蹤影了。牠從我們身邊跑走的時候，我們正帶著牠在中央森林公園溜達，現在牠可能還在那一帶逗留。牠失蹤時戴著棕色項圈。拜託大家，幫我們尋找查理！

• 查理是一隻大型混種犬，毛髮大部分是黃色的，但是全身上下散布著白色斑點，包括牠的尾巴尖端。牠大約40公斤重、50公分高。

- 查理喜歡吃零食、玩牠的玩具。牠不怕生，如果你叫查理的名字，牠就會跑到你身邊。牠喜歡認識新朋友，想要玩耍時會變得很活潑。

- 找到查理的人，將可獲得200美元酬謝。

- 如果您看到查理、或是覺得可能是牠的狗狗，請隨時來電 (432) 123-1234 或是透過推特帳號@joydog123傳訊息給我們。

我們非常擔心查理，因為牠不習慣在外流浪，我們希望查理能早點回家。

19 起死回生的 6 招 P. 56

當你發現有人倒在地上不省人事，你會怎麼做？以下六個簡單步驟，能幫助你拯救他人性命（譯注：即心肺復甦術CPR）。

步驟1：叫救護車
輕拍此人，詢問對方是否沒事。如果他／她沒有醒來，請立刻打電話叫救護車。

步驟2：將對方翻身成仰躺
請小心地幫對方翻身，呈背朝下仰躺姿。將他／她的頭後仰，使其嘴巴張開，觀察口腔內部，如有任何物品，請將其取出。

步驟3：檢查呼吸
將耳朵靠近對方的嘴邊，仔細聆聽，如果他／她還有呼吸，請靜候救護車抵達。如果聽了10秒鐘還是沒有聽見任何氣息，請繼續進行下列步驟。

步驟4：進行30次胸部按壓
將一隻手掌放在另一隻手掌上方，雙手重疊。用力且快速的在對方胸腔中央下壓，邊壓邊數30下。
（譯注：根據衛福部建議，若為成人，須於其兩乳頭連線中央下壓5至6公分，速度為每分鐘100–120 次。兒童或嬰兒另有標準。）

步驟5：進行兩次吹氣
將對方的頭往後傾，捏住他／她的鼻子、打開他／她的嘴巴，然後將你的嘴扣合對方的嘴並吹氣，應使對方胸腔有起伏動作。此步驟需進行兩次。（譯注：衛福部建議每口氣吹1秒鐘。）

步驟：6 重複
重複步驟4和步驟5，直到對方開始呼吸或是救護車抵達為止。

20 給蘿拉的影音訊息 P. 58

以下是大家傳給蘿拉的影音訊息

梅姬：蘿拉，我們從一年級就是好朋友，現在妳要到新的國家、就讀新學校了，祝福妳在那裡展開奇妙的旅程，但千萬別忘記我！記得喔，妳可以隨時打電話或傳訊息給我！祝妳在法國一帆風順！

史密斯老師：我知道搬到別的國家會讓人不安，但妳是個很聰明勇敢的女孩，想必很快就會適應新的語言和風俗。我和其他老師都祝你一切順利，希望妳將來能回來看看我們，告訴我們新生活裡發生的許多精彩故事！

艾咪姑姑：你爸爸告訴我，他要攜家帶眷搬到法國時，我氣到不行！我再也沒辦法每週末和我最疼愛的姪女見面了！但他向我保證說，不久後我就可以過去探望妳。我們可以一起去參觀各大美術館！我等不及了！

莎拉：妳就要離我而去了！妳不在的時候，我要抄誰的功課呢？但說實在的，我的好麻吉，沒有妳的話，學校生活會變得一團糟的。我親手做了這份禮物，讓妳戴了可以禦寒，同時也會想起我。把妳的地址傳給我吧，我再寄給妳！

Unit 2 字彙學習

認識同義字與反義字／從上下文推測字義

21 「疑惑」的人際問題 P. 62

有事問安妮 | 安妮‧史密斯每個月會為您解答疑難雜症……

問題1

親愛的安妮：

我有個問題。我身邊有些朋友開始在聊約會的話題，常會彼此討論自己喜歡的男生。但我現在真的不想跟人約會，我還是個國中生，覺得以後還會有很多時間可以約會，現在只想和朋友開心的相處，但我擔心，如果我不假裝對約會有興趣，他們會覺得我很奇怪，還會取笑我。我該怎麼做？

疑惑

安妮的回應：

親愛的「疑惑」：

你並不孤單。對許多青少年而言，這種問題屢見不鮮。有些人情竇初開的年齡比別人早，但即使現在還不想要投入這方面的事，也一點都不奇怪。事實上，我覺得以你現在的年紀來說，不想著談戀愛是件好事，這樣你就可以專注在別的事務上，像是你的學業、家人和愛好等。你說得沒錯，以後約會的時間多的是。你只要向朋友坦率表達你的感受就好，如果他們是好朋友，就不會為難你。

安妮

22 學生瑜伽：增強記憶力的兩招 P. 64

大考迫在眉睫，你正在熬夜挑燈夜戰。你已經仔細讀完所有筆記了，但是不知怎地，你就是記不住剛剛讀過的內容。這聽起來是不是讓你心有戚戚焉？很多學生都要想知道：我要如何在考前增強記憶力？答案是：瑜伽！

做瑜伽對你的身心健康都有所益處。研究顯示我們在做瑜伽時，大腦會獲得更多的氧氣，進而刺激你的記憶力，幫助你記憶更清晰。

你練習瑜伽時，身體也會釋放一種名叫「腦內啡」的化學物質，能提高你的專注力，你就能夠回想起更多讀過的筆記內容。此外，腦內啡也能讓你心情愉悅、學習效率更好！

請見下頁兩種能夠提升記憶力的姿勢。

魚式

姿勢步驟：

❶ 躺在地上，臉部朝上。
❷ 雙臂放在身體兩側。
❸ 用前臂的力量來幫助你挺胸。
❹ 頭向後仰，讓頭靠在墊子上。
❺ 保持雙腿、雙腳貼著地面。

英雄式

姿勢步驟：

❶ 雙膝併攏，雙腳分開地跪坐在地板上。
❷ 臀部端坐在兩腳之間。
❸ 保持背部挺直。
❹ 雙手合十放在胸前。

---

23 出售健身腳踏車！ P. 66

二手健身腳踏車熱賣中

· 型號：Superfit 3000
· 德國製
· 二手商品，但是貨況良好
· 可配送至波士頓各區。

價格：249.99美元（或價高者得）

問與答

問題1
Mike_C：嗨，這台看起來很不錯，但是可能有點太大，我的公寓會放不下。腳踏車的尺寸是多少呢？

回答：腳踏車的長度是1.5公尺，寬度是50公分。

問題2
Diane_M：可以問一下這台有多重嗎？我住的地方要爬樓梯，我擔心我搬不上去。

回答：重量是30公斤，應該算好搬，但如果你需要幫忙，我可以在送去給你的時候，幫你搬上樓。

問題3
Kiki_W：我的鄰居有些是長輩，對噪音很敏感。這台健身腳踏車使用時會很吵嗎？

回答：不會，一點也不。事實上，幾乎是靜悄悄的感覺。

問題4
Xiao_K：我看到健身車前方有台LED螢幕。上面會顯示什麼資訊？

回答：螢幕會顯示距離、速度、運動時間，還有燃燒的卡路里總量。

閱讀更多……

24 打造生涯閱讀力！ P. 68

多項研究顯示，經常手不釋卷能有助於激發想像力、增進記憶力並改善心理健康。但是如果你不是那種百無聊賴時，會自動自發拾起書本閱讀的人，養成規律的閱讀習慣可能會很困難。要是你想要提升閱讀量，以下有幾個方法可以一試。

首先，隨身都攜帶一本書。早上出門的時候，務必將一本有趣的讀物和你的學校用品一起放進書包。如此一來，但凡你有幾分鐘的空檔，手邊隨時都有書可以看。

其次，要寫閱讀日誌。每看完一本書，都做個筆記：什麼時候開始閱讀、什麼時候讀完、對這本書的看法為何、最喜歡書中哪幾句話等等。看到自己的閱讀書單日益增長，能夠激勵自己繼續保持這個習慣。

最後，不妨參與讀書社群。想要培養對閱讀的熱愛，一個絕佳方式就是結交其他同樣喜愛閱讀的人。參加讀書會吧，實體的讀書會或線上讀書會皆可，並跟別人分享你對所讀書籍的看法。透過這種方式，有關之後要讀哪些書，你也會獲得一些很好的建議！

25 難以下嚥的國民美食 P. 70

這個食物的味道比藍紋起司濃烈一百倍，聞起來滿是尿騷味。一位知名的電視節目主廚說，這是他吃過「味道最糟糕、最噁心、最難吃的東西」！對許多人而言，冰島發酵鯊魚肉「hákarl」也許聽起來令人卻步，但對冰島人而言，卻是深受喜愛的國民美食。

冰島發酵鯊魚肉是以格陵蘭鯊魚肉製成。這種鯊魚肉新鮮時吃下肚可能會致命，因此需要經過多道程序才可將其轉變為可食用的狀態。首先，將鯊魚肉放進地洞，以沙土和小石子覆蓋，接著再以大塊的重石壓住，擠出魚肉汁，如此壓製6至12週。之後取出鯊魚肉，吊掛風乾數月之久，接著就可以切塊食用。

食用冰島發酵鯊魚肉的歷史可追溯至一千多年前的維京時代。維京人透過此法料理鯊魚肉，確保在糧食短少時還有食物可以果腹。如今，雖然冰島人不再為食物短缺所苦，但享用發酵鯊魚肉是他們和過去歷史連結的獨特方式。

26 湖邊驚魂記 P. 72

我真不敢相信上週末發生了什麼事！我跟家人到野外露營的時候，經歷了一件非比尋常的事情。

那時我跟家人去斯努根湖露營，我爸媽搭帳篷時，我跟我哥去湖邊探險，想看看附近有什麼東西。我們看到一大叢灌木叢，還聽到叢中傳來怪聲，我們決定一探究竟，於是躡手躡腳地靠近灌木叢，原本打算一聲不響地接近，不想驚動可能躲在裡面的小動物。這時，我哥居然咳嗽了一下！一隻大鵝隨即從灌木叢裡衝了出來，一邊發出恐怖的叫聲，而且朝我迎面而來！我轉身全速逃跑，可是那隻大鵝一直瘋狂拍打著翅膀，一邊追著我不放。我找了棵樹，迅速地爬到樹上，幸好那隻鵝沒有跟著爬上來，而是決定走開。

我最好研究一下遇到鵝發飆時要怎麼應付，下次就能有備無患。我以前都不知道，鵝居然也能這麼兇猛！

27 農場參訪一日遊 P. 74

希爾谷中學通知單

2022年3月3日

陽光谷農場校外教學

親愛的家長：

八年級的學生即將到陽光谷農場進行校外教學。全體參加學生會在學校外面集合，然後搭乘校車前往農場。

抵達該地點後，學生可以餵食動物，午餐後則將學習如何種植稻米、玉米等農作物，這提供給學生很好的機會，可以體驗農場的生活方式，並且更了解農民每天的工作內容。當天放學前，將由校車將學生送回學校。

日期：4月6日（星期三）
時間：上午8:00–下午3:30
地點：陽光谷農場

請為您的孩子準備午餐，因為農場沒有販賣餐點。我們建議學生當天穿著體育服，並著耐穿、合適的鞋子。欲報名參加者，請填寫本通知單所附的報名表並繳回，以便我們掌握有多少學生會參加校外教學。我們希望每位學生在這次參訪中，都能玩得開心又盡興。

教師 埃文斯 敬上

28 學習生活技能 P. 76

如何「轉大人」：給青少年的指南

張肯尼 著

前言

各位現在都是個青少年，每天都得待在學校好幾個小時，會擔心成績，並為交友關係而困擾。我知道青少年的生活相當不容易，但很快地，你就會長大成人，而且我敢跟你保證，日子不會變得比較輕鬆！身為一個成年人，你會面臨排山倒海而來的責任。你得要自行打理食、衣需求，還必須支付房租等，諸如此類，不勝枚舉。過去我歷經青少年到成人的轉變時，就感到這個過程令人幾乎招架不住！

我在這本書想要教給各位青少年讀者的是，一切我在你們這個年紀時，恨不得早就懂得的技能。如果你現在就學起來，那麼在成年後，你會過得更游刃有餘。

當然，我無法回答所有的人生難題，比如：「生命的意義為何？」，但是我可以教你怎麼省錢、怎麼購買食品雜貨、怎麼準備健康的三餐、怎麼舉辦有趣的派對等更多其他疑難雜症！

希望各位讀完本書後，會大大覺得更有自信、更勇於獨立，而等你終於長大成人時，就不會像我當年一樣，感到迷茫不知所措了。

29 有話要說？貼在布告欄吧！ P. 78

英文需要協助嗎？我要找人救我數學！

或許我們可以互相幫忙。

我可以協助你解決各種困難的文法問題，並一起提升你的英語寫作能力。

而你可以來教我理解棘手的數學主題。

也許我們可以約午餐時間或是放學後見面。請寄電子郵件到我的信箱：mathenglishswap@gmail.com

金珍妮，8年級

烘焙社

你希望自己是烘焙達人嗎？
來報名加入烘焙社吧。
與你相約每週三午餐時間見。
如果你想加入，請到203教室
向朴老師洽詢！
我們會做各式各樣美味的蛋糕
跟餅乾，你可以跟朋友分享，
也可以帶回家喔！

科幻小說大拍賣

我哥哥要搬到外面住了，他想把許多舊的科幻小說出清掉。

書本眾多可供選擇，每本只要1.5美元！要出售的小說書單可在以下網址查詢：www.mybrothersbooks.freesites.com

有興趣的話，請透過以上網站發訊息給我，或在下課時間找我聊聊。

崔肯尼，9年級

30 社交距離：不只救人命，蜜蜂也跟風 P. 80

大家聽到「社交距離」一詞，腦海裡想到的大概是COVID-19，但你知道人類並非地球上唯一利用保持社交距離來維持健康的動物嗎？

蜜蜂同樣採取社交距離的措施：你可以發現到，較年輕的蜜蜂會在蜂巢中央照顧幼蜂和女王蜂，而較年長的蜜蜂則大多是在蜂巢的外圍區域，其任務是從外頭的植物中覓食並帶回蜂巢。出外覓食會使較年長的蜜蜂曝露在更多健康風險之下，而蜂巢內這兩類蜂群保持距離的做法，意在減少雙方接觸，有助於保護蜂巢裡最寶貴的成員。

而感染瓦蟎（譯注：又稱蜂蟹蟎）的蜂群甚至會擴大社交距離。當蜂巢中出現這些不速之客，蜜蜂會加強保持社交距離。覓食蜂會遷移到更靠近蜂巢外側的區域，較年輕的蜜蜂則會更靠近蜂巢中心。蜜蜂也會減少覓食間飛舞的習性，因為此舉會使瓦蟎擴散。如果沒有這些保持社交距離的措施，蜂群可能會日益衰弱而無法生存，所以社交距離無論是對巢中的蜜蜂、或是都市的人類來說，都是救命良策！

3-1 影像圖表

31 跨年夜交通管制 P. 84 ....

每年的跨年夜是充滿歡樂卻又繁忙不已的時刻,許多人會舉辦派對來慶祝,有些城市甚至會施放煙火表演。十二點的鐘聲響起時,大家都會到外頭欣賞煙火照亮夜空。因此,街上可能會湧進成千上萬的人潮,市府單位也就必須實施特別措施來封閉道路。通常進行交通管制的路段僅限跨年煙火地點周邊,時間只會在午夜前後幾個小時,這樣就不會過度妨礙交通。

格林市每逢跨年夜都會舉行煙火表演,煙火施放的地點就在市中心的格林塔。每年格林市政府都會公告地圖,告知民眾哪些道路會在夜間封閉。這類地圖會標示每條道路的名稱,並用不同顏色的線條標示哪些道路將會封閉。

**格林市跨年煙火表演
交通管制規定**

為了安全起見,所記區域將在以下時段禁止車輛通行。

紅色區域
12月31日(一)晚上8時至10時

藍色區域
12月31日(一)晚上10時
至1月1日(二)凌晨3時

32 運動時間到! P. 86 ....

如果你住在大城市,適合運動的地方可能一處難求。一到戶外,車輛來來往往,而且空氣品質差,吸入有害健康。但是如果運氣好,你家附近正巧就有運動中心,中心裡有許多完善的設施,能讓民眾在安全的環境中做運動。

運動中心白天也常會開設課程,讓男女老少都能在老師的指導下學習運動項目,課程可能包括瑜伽課、游泳課、桌球課等等。你可以在運動中心的課程表,找到這些課程的詳細資訊,課程表(如上所示)會顯示出每週的上課時間,也應會包含收費以及班級人數限制等細節。

你何不到附近的運動中心,索取一份課程表呢?看一看有沒有你感興趣的課程,或許就能發掘新的運動,成為你的最愛!

時段／日期	週一	週二	週三	週四	週五	週六	週日
格林市運動中心　午晚課程表（**9月1日前適用**）							
下午4–5點	羽毛球(未滿16歲)	游泳(未滿16歲)	攀岩(未滿16歲)	瑜伽(未滿16歲)	羽毛球(未滿16歲)	桌球(未滿16歲)	攀岩(未滿16歲)
下午5–6點	游泳(成人)	羽毛球(成人)	游泳(未滿16歲)	羽毛球(未滿16歲)	攀岩(未滿16歲)	游泳(未滿16歲)	桌球(成人)
晚上6–7點	攀岩(成人)	瑜伽(未滿16歲)	桌球(未滿16歲)	游泳(成人)	瑜伽(未滿16歲)	攀岩(成人)	瑜伽(成人)
晚上7–8點	瑜伽(成人)	攀岩(成人)	羽毛球(成人)	桌球(未滿16歲)	桌球(成人)	羽毛球(成人)	游泳(成人)
晚上8–9點	桌球(成人)	攀岩(成人)	瑜伽(成人)	桌球(成人)	游泳(成人)	瑜伽(成人)	羽毛球(成人)

*如欲報名課程，請至服務台洽詢。
未滿16歲課程：每小時10美元　成人班：每小時18美元　每班人數限20人。

33 美食外送「疫」軍突起　P. 88

受到新冠疫情的影響，2020年對許多行業來說是慘澹經營的一年，但是有項產業卻在這一年間異軍突起，那就是「美食外送」。由於許多餐廳暫停開放內用，民眾因此轉而使用美食外送應用程式，將餐點直送到府。

2020年期間，即使台灣的餐廳都還繼續營業，美食外送服務依然大有斬獲。許多台灣民眾因為不願群聚，轉而用外送程式。將餐點外送到家裡不失是好辦法，可以避開人群，也能降低感染COVID-19的風險。

在一項調查中，台灣網友被問到了2020年上半年美食外送的使用習慣。下一頁的圓餅圖顯示了他們的回答。圓餅圖是將圓形或餅形切成數個區塊來表示數量，數量愈大，在圓餅內所占的區塊也愈大。如你所見，將近11%網友是在2020年上半年，首度使用外送送餐到家！真可說是數量爆增！

2020年上半年美食外送服務使用習慣調查

（來源：資策會產業情報研究所）

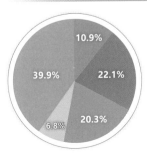

10.9%
39.9%
22.1%
6.8%
20.3%

- 未曾在新冠疫情前訂過美食外送，但在2020年上半年開始下單
- 新冠疫情前就訂過美食外送，且在2020年上半年增加下單次數
- 新冠疫情前就訂過美食外送，但在2020年上半年下單次數未增加
- 新冠疫情前就訂過美食外送，但在2020年上半年未曾下單
- 未曾在新冠疫情前訂過美食外送，且在2020年上半年未曾下單

34 生活成本大哉問 P. 90 ....

你想不想有天到國外居住？在異國生活是個很棒的經歷，確實能提高對世界的認識，對你的成長很有助益。在你決定要住在哪個國家之前，有件很重要的事情需要考慮，那就是「生活成本」。

生活成本是指為了重要的日常所需，必須支出的金額，包括房租、食物、水電瓦斯等費用。事實上，上述三者就占據了大城市生活所需的大半生

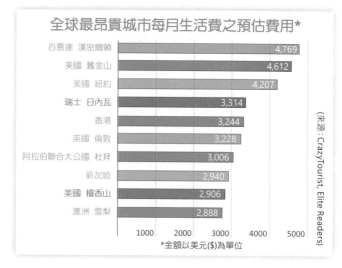

活開銷，但也要考慮到其他項目，像是治裝費、交通費、娛樂費等。

請看下頁的長條圖，圖中顯示的是全球生活費最高的幾座城市。長條圖是以不同長度的直條來表示數字，而數字愈大，直條就愈長，以方便比較各項數字。

35 有朋自遠方來 P. 92

台灣的美景、美食與人情味，都是台灣備受觀光客青睞的原因。COVID-19疫情爆發前，每年來台的人數逐年增長。2010年有570萬名旅客赴台，至2019年旅客數就突破了1100萬人次！

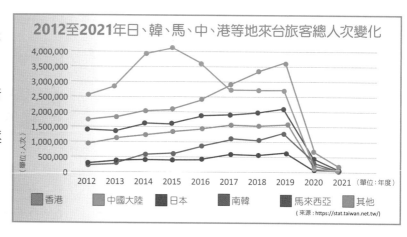

來台的旅客大多來自亞洲

各地，例如中國大陸、香港、日本、南韓和馬來西亞。這些地區往來台灣的飛行時間短，且機票便宜，旅客也喜歡台灣治安良好、物美價廉，以及輕鬆悠閒的氣氛。

下頁的折線圖顯示上述五個地方的來台旅客人次。折線圖是以小點來標記數字，然後以線條連接各點。藉由觀察折線的波動，就能看出數字隨著時間變化向上或向下的走勢。人次數據始於2012年，於2021年結束。2020年時，台灣因為新冠疫情而停止開放觀光客入境，即是過去兩年來人次驟降的原因。

3-2 參考資料

36 戰火不斷的時代 P. 94 ....

2022年，俄羅斯向鄰國烏克蘭發動攻擊，舉世震驚。21世紀未過一半，就已經有數場大型戰爭爆發。上世紀末，許多人期望新世紀會更和平。20世紀這百年間，爆發了許多慘無人道的戰爭。

在第一次和第二次世界大戰期間，世界各國紛紛捲入戰爭，相互交戰，這在20世紀前是前所未聞之事，更有許多血流成河的地方戰爭，同國人民相互廝殺，西班牙內戰與國共內戰只是其中兩例。

請看下頁的時間軸。時間軸會將事件按發生的先後順序列出來，此處時間軸顯示的是近代重大戰爭，上方列出年代，下方則標示出戰爭名稱，而從紫色的條狀區塊，可以得知每場大戰持續了多長時間。讓我們期許21世紀不會重蹈上世紀的覆轍吧。

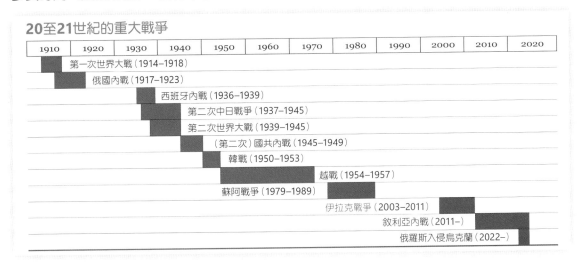

20至21世紀的重大戰爭

1910	1920	1930	1940	1950	1960	1970	1980	1990	2000	2010	2020

第一次世界大戰（1914–1918）
俄國內戰（1917–1923）
西班牙內戰（1936–1939）
第二次中日戰爭（1937–1945）
第二次世界大戰（1939–1945）
（第二次）國共內戰（1945–1949）
韓戰（1950–1953）
越戰（1954–1957）
蘇阿戰爭（1979–1989）
伊拉克戰爭（2003–2011）
敘利亞內戰（2011–）
俄羅斯入侵烏克蘭（2022–）

---

37 蟲蟲滿天下！ P. 96

昆蟲的身影隨處可見：廚房裡有螞蟻、花盆周圍有蜜蜂、垃圾桶裡有蒼蠅。事實上，科學家認為，地球上大約90%的動物都是昆蟲！

昆蟲何以如此得天獨厚？其中一個原因就是體積。昆蟲身形短小，意味其生存所需的能量較少，也更容易躲避危險。昆蟲體積雖小，卻身強體壯，所有昆蟲的體表都有堅韌的外骨骼，可以保護自己免於受傷。昆蟲有這麼多優勢集於一身，難怪有辦法主宰世界！

市面上有許多優良讀物，能讓你更深入了解昆蟲。選購好書時，請先瀏覽開頭的目錄。（此處以《探究昆蟲世界》一書為例）。目錄會標示出每一章的名稱以及從哪一頁開始，翻閱目錄可以讓你充分了解是否會對此書感興趣。

探究昆蟲世界

目錄

---

38 摺紙的藝術 P. 98

日本的摺紙藝術（譯注：日文原文為「折り紙」，羅馬拼音作「origami」，現已納入英語詞彙）十分易於說明，你只需要一張紙、一點耐心即可。藉由不斷摺疊紙張，就能創造出美麗的造型。

要摺成什麼，都可以任意發揮，但最常見的是動物。有些基本款（例如大家流行摺的紙鶴）轉眼間就能摺好。然而，較困難的形狀則需要很多技巧，而且需投入大量時間才能完成。

你想多了解摺紙的歷史嗎？還是你想自己學會摺紙？如果是的話，網路搜尋引擎會是個很好的著手點。你在搜尋資訊時，會得到一連串的搜尋結果，每筆結果的上方會顯示網址，下方則會列有部分細節，告訴你可從該網站找到何種資訊。此處列出的是在搜尋引擎輸入「origami」後，可能得到的結果範例。

www.how-to-origami.com
今天開始學摺紙
學會怎麼摺出眾多酷炫的造型吧。每種摺紙造型都附有清楚的步驟說明和示意圖。請到我們的資料庫，查看從基礎到高難度、超過一千種摺紙設計的教學！

www.everythingjapan.com.jp/origami/history
摺紙藝術的故事
摺紙藝術在日本擁有悠久的歷史。摺紙藝術的文字紀錄首次出現在井原西鶴於1680年所寫的詩句，其中談到了一種經常用於婚禮的紙蝴蝶設計……

www.origamiforkids.com
超過30種簡單、可愛的摺紙設計
歡迎來看看我們超過30種的摺紙設計，小朋友能輕鬆上手，而且還超級可愛！造型包括兔子、青蛙、泰迪熊等等！

www.thepaperstore.com/origami-paper
各種尺寸和色系的摺紙專用紙
您在找摺紙專用紙嗎？我們的商品選擇多元、價格實惠，而且紙質輕薄易摺……

www.localteacher.com/arts/origami
找尋離你最近的摺紙老師
現在報名摺紙課，每小時鐘點費只需15美元。第一堂課均免費，歡迎各種程度的學員報名參加。

39 別憂心，要開心！ P. 100

你快樂嗎？這是個單純卻又重要的問題。研究顯示，快樂的人工作表現較佳、身體更健康，而且累積的財富更多。簡言之，如果你常保心情愉快，人生通常就能過得更順利美好。而且，快樂的人往往也會讓他人感到快樂，然後這些人又為更多人帶來快樂，以此類推，因此快樂不僅對你有好處，更能造福所有人！

在英文裡，「happy」有很多種表達方法，例如 joyful（喜悅）、cheery（愉快）、merry（歡樂）或 sunny（開朗），不一而足。想知道所有可用來形容自己「happy」的表達方法，就去查「索引典」吧。索引典有點像字典，從中查詢一個詞時，不僅會了解該詞詞義，還可看到一連串同義詞與反義詞。同義詞是指意義雷同的詞；反義詞是指意義相反的詞，而索引典每筆詞條會依A到Z的順序列出同義詞和反義詞。

happy

1. [形] 感受或表現出歡樂
   ・擁有許多好友，讓傑克感到非常快樂。
   同義詞：幸福的、開心的、愉快的、歡欣
   的、高興的、喜悅的、歡樂的、
   欣喜的、滿意的、開朗的、感恩的
   反義詞：不滿的、不悅的、傷心的、
   不快樂的

2. [形] 願意做某事
   ・超市員工總是樂於協助顧客。
   同義詞：滿足的、歡欣的、高興的、
   欣喜的、準備好的、願意的
   反義詞：不情願的、不願意的

3. [形] 幸運且便利
   ・我們兩人今天在公園碰到面，就像
   幸運的巧合。
   同義詞：便利的、巧妙的、幸運的、
   好運的、湊巧的、及時的
   反義詞：不便的、不湊巧的、不幸的、
   倒楣的、不適時的

40 夏日輕食趣 P. 102

炎炎夏日，你最不想吃到的是重口味又熱氣騰騰的餐點吧！沒錯，你想吃清爽、解膩又新鮮的菜色！

我在夏季很愛做的一道料理就是「彩虹沙拉」，做法超簡單，而且美味又健康！這道料理的精神在於盡量使用多種不同顏色的食材，這樣就能在品嚐不同風味之餘，還能攝取到大量有益健康的維生素。

你喜歡的各類蔬菜都可以用來做彩虹沙拉，不過這個食譜是我很喜歡做的一種，用的是在地市場可找到的簡單食材，並以美味的花生醬來做沙拉醬，為料理增添更多風味。食譜上列出了做這道沙拉所需的一切食材，並循序漸進地引導你完成料理。光是看食譜，就讓我垂涎不已！敬請慢用！

夏日彩虹沙拉

分量：4人份
製作時間：40分鐘
食材：

花生沙拉醬
• 3大匙無顆粒花生醬
• 3大匙巴薩米克醋
• 2大匙橄欖油
• 1小撮鹽
• 1小撮黑胡椒

沙拉
• 1顆生菜（萵苣）
• ¼ 顆紫甘藍
• 250克小番茄
• 1根中型紅蘿蔔
• 1條中型小黃瓜
• 50克黑豆
• 1顆黃甜椒
• ½ 顆紅洋蔥
• 1把新鮮羅勒
• 2大匙綜合堅果

步驟

1 將生菜、羅勒、紫甘藍、紅蘿蔔、小黃瓜、紅洋蔥、番茄和甜椒切一切。將所有蔬菜、黑豆和綜合堅果一起放進大碗。

2 將沙拉醬的所有食材放入小碗裡，並混調均勻。

3 將沙拉醬和沙拉放進冰箱30分鐘，好好冰鎮所有食材。

4 半小時後，再將沙拉醬加到沙拉裡，然後混拌均勻。

5 上菜開動！

4-1 閱讀技巧複習

41 客家人「補天穿」 P. 106 ....

客家人在台灣以勤奮精神為人所知,但在一個特別的日子裡,客家人會放下手邊工作,並歡唱山歌來慶祝。這天就是「天穿日」(譯注:又稱「補天節」),客家人會放假一天,來向拯救世界的女媧女神表示敬意。

根據華人傳說,水神(譯注:即共工)曾與火神(譯注:即祝融,另有說法稱衝突是因共工和顓頊爭帝而起)展開大戰。水神打了敗仗後,一頭撞向支撐天空的柱子上,柱子因而倒塌,使天空出現裂口,導致了人間發生可怕的災害。女神女媧的出現,讓看似失控的局面有了轉機。女媧迅速採取行動,以五色石填補天空的裂縫,使天空再次完好無缺,人間恢復祥和。

「天穿日」據說就是當年補天的日子。為了慶祝女媧補天,客家人(譯注:以北部客家人居多)常在這天一起去寺廟。大家都吃著糯米做的「甜粄」,象徵五色石;炸糯米球「油堆子」則會以針線裝飾,象徵女媧使用的工具。

傳統上,天穿日落在農曆正月20日,台灣過去將這天訂為「全國客家日」加以慶祝(全國客家日現已調整至國曆12月28日,即1988年「還我客家話運動」的發起日)。台灣政府設立此特殊節日,意在向客家人致敬。

42 讓世界豐衣足食 P. 108 ....

現今全球約有八億人深受飢餓之苦,而「世界糧食計劃署」(WFP)就是一個致力減少各地飢餓人口的組織。目前WFP的服務對象涵蓋117國的飢餓人民,其主要業務之一,即是將緊急糧食送到受波及的戰地人民手中。

WFP相信戰爭和飢荒密不可分。一旦爆發戰爭,許多人就會被迫遷離家園和故土。人民失去了可供種植糧食的土地、又沒有錢購買食物,就更有可能挨餓。然而,飢餓往往也是戰爭的導火線,如果人民因為挨餓而心懷怨懟,就更有可能訴諸暴力,因此解決飢餓問題,是讓世界邁向和平的重要一步。

為了達成此目標,WFP努力為世界各地的貧苦地區定期提供糧食。戰端一起,WFP就會提供食物給身陷戰火的人民;戰爭結束後,WFP也會留下來幫助人民重建生活。WFP也因其盡心盡力,於2020年獲頒諾貝爾和平獎。從WFP諸多的付出來看,得獎確實當之無愧!

43 碧海中的奧祕 P. 110 ....

大家也許聽說過,宇宙深處存在著不可思議的暗物質:「黑洞」,但你有聽過「藍洞」嗎?雖然藍洞和我們的距離接近許多,但同樣很不可思議喔。

海洋裡可以找到許多深邃、垂直的洞穴，這就是「藍洞」。從上方俯瞰，藍洞看起來是一圈深藍水域，被開闊的淺藍色海域包裹其中，但是藍洞深度可下探數百公尺。全世界最深的藍洞，就位在越南與菲律賓之間的南海上，深度超過300公尺！可以想見，藍洞是潛水愛好者的熱門去處，不過到藍洞潛水可能會有致命的危險。有個位於埃及的藍洞，因為有超過40名潛水客在此喪生，而被稱為「潛水者之墓」。

藍洞不僅是潛水人的熱門據點，也廣泛受到科學家的關注。藍洞裡的自然環境非常有意思，洞底幾乎沒有光線或氧氣，但是諸如細菌等微生物，仍能存在於這類幽暗的環境。科學家可透過研究此類生物，探究生存條件與地球迥然不同的其他星球上，可能會有的生命樣貌。

44 人生的下一步 P. 112

P. 112

親愛的麥克叔叔：

我遇到了一個難題，想請教叔叔：明年我就要從國中畢業，但還不確定接下來該何去何從。我應該去讀普通高中，接著升大學嗎？還是該去讀高職或五年制專科學校呢？普通高中的課程比較偏學術性，高職或五專的課程則側重實務。我父母希望我去讀普通高中，但我熱愛和汽車打交道，我認為在高職或五專能受到更完善的培訓，未來能從事我真正想做的行業。我該選擇哪條路呢？

羅伊

親愛的羅伊：

這是很好的問題，看你這麼認真思考升學方向，我很欣慰。如你所知，我目前從事導遊工作，這份工作很棒。我帶領來自世界各地的遊客，參觀台灣的美景。我自己就是五專出身，而且並不後悔，當時我學到很多很棒的技能，幫助我得到這份夢寐以求的工作。如果你對自己未來職涯有很明確的想法，那就去讀能驅動你追尋夢想的學校吧。

希望我有幫上忙！

麥克叔叔

4-2 字彙學習複習

45 讀書配音樂，可以嗎？ P. 114

P. 114

很多學生喜歡邊聽音樂邊讀書，但這麼做會有幫助嗎？聽音樂會不會使你更難記住需要學習的內容？聽音樂和讀書有可能同時進行嗎？

音樂能讓你感到放鬆、心情變好，也能幫助你忘掉作業的壓力，或者讓你在備考期間舒緩緊張。音樂也有助於你在長時間讀書時堅持下去，因為聽音樂能為讀書這個活動增添愉快的氣氛。

沒有歌詞的音樂，似乎對學生的記憶影響不大，然而有歌詞的音樂則會讓人分心，更難專注於學業上。此外，音量太大或節奏太快的音樂，也會在你準備考試時影響你的記憶力。

如果你想要邊聽音樂邊讀書，就要慎選音樂的種類。請勿選擇會讓你更讀不下書的音樂。你可以嘗試聽一些寧靜、輕柔的古典樂，既能幫助你放鬆，同時又能讓你集中精神。

46 網路交友危機四伏？ P. 116

艾娃：還記得我跟妳說過的那款交友APP嗎？我已經在上面建好個人檔案了！

瓊：認真的嗎，艾娃？我還真以為我們上次聊過後，妳已經決定不去嘗試了！

艾娃：別擔心，瓊。我還沒開始約會——目前啦。

瓊：好吧，如果妳真想這麼做，一定要答應我幾件事。

艾娃：好喔，老媽。

瓊：妳要慶幸我不是妳媽！

艾娃：我完全知道妳要講什麼：不要用真名、不要把地址告訴別人，噢，還有不要分享任何不想讓父母看到的照片。

瓊：對，但還有更多要注意的，不見得每個人都會透露真面目。

艾娃：妳要放輕鬆點，瓊。

瓊：放輕鬆？要是最後妳跟某個危險份子去約會了怎麼辦？妳想在尋覓愛情途中被殺害嗎？或是被騙光所有的錢？這種事情層出不窮，艾娃，我怎麼可能放鬆得了？

艾娃：好啦，好啦！我有聽進去。

瓊：我今天早上讀到一篇文章，上面說經查發現，使用線上交友的年輕女性，有近兩成曾受過肢體暴力的威脅。

艾娃：好可怕。也許我在嘗試前應該要再多想想。

瓊：好加在！

47 失火了！注意濃煙！ P. 118

雖然大火足以致命，但有更多人命是葬送在濃煙之下。事實上，一般認為在火災事故裡，有5至8成的罹難者是因吸入濃煙而不治。

如果受困在濃煙瀰漫的室內，你知道該如何因應嗎？一般來說，消防單位會建議壓低身體，但不要太低。由於比重較重的有毒氣體會下沉到靠近地面的地方，所以你應該要以雙手跟雙膝代步，往門口方向移動。眼睛視線要跟著牆根走，這樣就能盡快找到房門。

有傳言說，逃生時應以濕毛巾摀住嘴巴。然而，布料並不能防止致命氣體滲入，因此切勿浪費時間尋找濕的覆蓋物，盡量讓你的呼吸能淺則淺即可。

到達門邊時，不要立刻開門。先檢查有沒有濃煙從下方的門縫冒出，然後迅速地用手摸一下，看看有多燙。如果火勢已經蔓延到門後，那就不是安全的出口，此時應掉頭爬向窗戶。

即使吸入少量濃煙，也會導致你生病或失去意識，所以切記，在濃煙密布的房間裡，務必分秒必爭。

48 天搖地動上演中 P. 120

你正呼呼大睡之際，突然驚醒過來，發現房間來回的搖晃，就像電影中的情節一樣。你愣了一下，才明白當前的狀況，然後你只感到更糟糕，因為你正身陷一場大地震中。

對於生活在台灣的人而言，地震可說是家常便飯。台灣這座島嶼每年會經歷大約一千次有感地震，幾乎一天三次。原因為何呢？因為催生台灣本島形成的，正是會引發地震的海底板塊運動。在台灣東邊，菲律賓海板塊被推拉到歐亞板塊下方；而另一方面在南邊，歐亞板塊則被推拉到菲律賓海板塊下方。這兩股板塊運動，正好就在台灣下方形成活躍的碰撞帶，因此導致地震不斷。

也有研究顯示，地震和陸地的儲水量之間可能有關。科學家發現，許多強震發生在台灣的乾季，也就是2月到4月，而在雨季尾聲的7月到9月，地震最不活躍。因此我們小小的台灣島，或許在天搖地動的地震方面，可說是腹背受敵！

4-3 影像圖表複習

49 撞名運動大不同 P. 122

美國人在說他們熱愛「football」時，說的通常是球員需要戴上頭盔、並用丟擲或腳踢一顆橢圓小球的運動。在這項運動中，球員的目標在於把球推進到球場遠端的得分區（譯注：稱為達陣區或端區〔end zone〕）。不過，對於世界其他地方的人而言，「football」的定義卻十分不同，指的是球員必須將圓球踢進球門來得分的運動。為了避免混淆，前者通常被稱為「美式足球」（American football），後者則稱為「足球」（soccer）。

要了解這兩種熱門運動之間的異同處，請看下頁的文氏圖。文氏圖有兩個圓圈，在下頁的文氏圖中，左圈列出的是美式足球的事實資訊；右圈列出的是足球的事實資訊，而中央兩圈交集處則列出美式足球與足球的共同處。

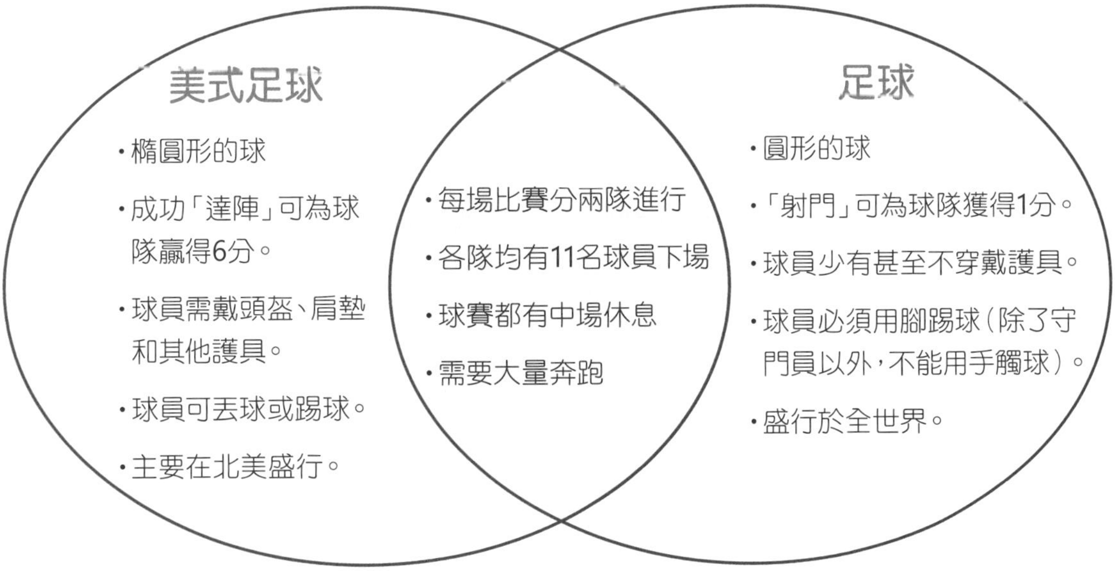

美式足球
- 橢圓形的球
- 成功「達陣」可為球隊贏得6分。
- 球員需戴頭盔、肩墊和其他護具。
- 球員可丟球或踢球。
- 主要在北美盛行。

（交集）
- 每場比賽分兩隊進行
- 各隊均有11名球員下場
- 球賽都有中場休息
- 需要大量奔跑

足球
- 圓形的球
- 「射門」可為球隊獲得1分。
- 球員少有甚至不穿戴護具。
- 球員必須用腳踢球（除了守門員以外，不能用手觸球）。
- 盛行於全世界。

50 縱橫古今看藝術 P. 124 ....

人類創作藝術的歷史已有數萬年。起初人類會在洞穴壁面上繪製動物的圖像。過了很久之後，古希臘人以金屬和石塊為眾多神祇製作了美麗的雕像。在古代中國，人們則在長畫卷上繪製鉅細靡遺的人物、山水畫。在19世紀的法國，藝術家們嘗試畫出光線本身變化多端的色彩與其光影作用。當然，例子不勝枚舉，此處僅略舉一二。

要想更全面地了解人類藝術史，何不閱讀藝術史主題的書籍呢？一本優質的藝術史書會涵蓋從古至今的藝術發展，讓你充分了解藝術是如何隨著時間變化的。

如果想找特定主題，可以查閱書末的索引。索引表會從A到Z的順序，列出書中的主題以及相對應的頁數，方便你查找閱讀。下頁是《縱橫古今看藝術》一書中的一小部分索引內容。

《縱橫古今看藝術》 索引（第 5 部分）

P

攝影	401–3
巴勃羅·畢卡索	572–7
傑克遜·波洛克	392
普普藝術	608–10
史前藝術 請參閱「洞穴藝術」	

Q

秦始皇，中國皇帝	633-5

R

拉斐爾	277
林布蘭	267
文藝復興	212–348
羅馬藝術	71–5
浪漫主義	314
俄羅斯藝術	362, 388

S

科學與藝術	623, 627

自畫像	132, 169, 248, 272, 331
靜物畫	290, 355, 383
超現實主義	389–92

T

大溪地	540–1
兵馬俑	411–13
提香	230–2
圖騰柱	25
J.M.W. 特納	325

Answer Key

Unit 1　閱讀技巧

1	1.B	2.C	3.C	4.D	5.B	**11**	1.B	2.D	3.A	4.C	5.B
2	1.B	2.A	3.D	4.C	5.C	**12**	1.A	2.D	3.C	4.B	5.A
3	1.C	2.C	3.B	4.D	5.A	**13**	1.D	2.C	3.A	4.B	5.D
4	1.B	2.D	3.B	4.D	5.A	**14**	1.A	2.B	3.C	4.D	5.C
5	1.C	2.A	3.D	4.B	5.C	**15**	1.C	2.D	3.B	4.B	5.A
6	1.D	2.B	3.A	4.C	5.A	**16**	1.C	2.B	3.A	4.C	5.B
7	1.C	2.A	3.C	4.B	5.D	**17**	1.A	2.D	3.D	4.B	5.C
8	1.B	2.D	3.A	4.C	5.D	**18**	1.B	2.A	3.C	4.D	5.A
9	1.C	2.D	3.A	4.C	5.B	**19**	1.A	2.B	3.C	4.C	5.D
10	1.A	2.C	3.C	4.B	5.D	**20**	1.D	2.A	3.A	4.D	5.B

Unit 2　字彙學習

21	1.B	2.C	3.A	4.B	5.D	**26**	1.B	2.A	3.D	4.C	5.B
22	1.C	2.A	3.D	4.D	5.B	**27**	1.A	2.A	3.C	4.A	5.C
23	1.D	2.A	3.C	4.A	5.B	**28**	1.C	2.C	3.A	4.D	5.A
24	1.A	2.C	3.B	4.D	5.C	**29**	1.A	2.B	3.D	4.A	5.C
25	1.C	2.B	3.C	4.D	5.A	**30**	1.D	2.C	3.A	4.D	5.A

Unit 3　學習策略

31	1.A	2.B	3.B	4.B	5.D	**36**	1.D	2.A	3.C	4.A	5.A
32	1.A	2.C	3.D	4.C	5.B	**37**	1.C	2.A	3.D	4.B	5.A
33	1.D	2.C	3.B	4.B	5.B	**38**	1.B	2.A	3.D	4.C	5.D
34	1.B	2.D	3.B	4.A	5.C	**39**	1.C	2.C	3.A	4.C	5.B
35	1.C	2.A	3.D	4.C	5.B	**40**	1.B	2.D	3.C	4.B	5.A

Unit 4　綜合練習

41	1.D	2.B	3.A	4.B	5.D	**46**	1.D	2.B	3.C	4.A	5.A
42	1.D	2.B	3.A	4.B	5.C	**47**	1.D	2.A	3.A	4.D	5.B
43	1.C	2.D	3.A	4.C	5.C	**48**	1.B	2.D	3.C	4.B	5.A
44	1.B	2.D	3.C	4.A	5.B	**49**	1.C	2.A	3.C	4.B	5.D
45	1.A	2.A	3.C	4.D	5.C	**50**	1.D	2.A	3.B	4.C	5.C

讀出英語核心素養 ③
九大技巧打造閱讀力

作者	Owain Mckimm ／
	Rob Webb（第 14, 18, 26, 27, 45 課）／ Ruth Chong（第 2, 22 課）／
	Shara Dupuis（第 30, 46 課）／ Richard Luhrs（第 48 課）／
	Laura Phelps（第 47 課）／ Kim Weiners（第 41 課）
譯者	黃詩韻／劉嘉珮
審訂	Helen Yeh
企畫編輯	葉俞均
編輯	高誀軒
主編	丁宥暄
校對	黃詩韻／許嘉華
內頁設計	草禾豐視覺設計有限公司／洪伊珊（中譯）
封面設計	林書玉
發行人	黃朝萍
製程管理	洪巧玲
出版者	寂天文化事業股份有限公司
電話	02-2365-9739
傳真	02-2365-9835
網址	www.icosmos.com.tw
讀者服務	onlineservice@icosmos.com.tw
出版日期	2022 年 6 月 初版一刷
	（寂天雲隨身聽 APP 版）
郵撥帳號	1998620-0 寂天文化事業股份有限公司

訂書金額未滿 1000 元，請外加運費 100 元。

〔若有破損，請寄回更換，謝謝〕

國家圖書館出版品預行編目 (CIP) 資料

讀出英語核心素養 . 3：九大技巧打造
閱讀力（寂天雲隨身聽 APP 版)/Owain
Mckimm 著；黃詩韻，劉嘉珮譯 . -- 初版 .
-- [臺北市]：寂天文化事業股份有限公司，
2022.06

面； 公分

ISBN 978-626-300-135-0(16K 平裝)

1.CST: 英語 2.CST: 讀本

805.18　　　　　　　　　　111008240